# To Chase A Ghost

by Harold Stromberger

No part of this book may be reproduced in any form or by any electronic or mechanical means, including information storage and retrieval systems – except in the case of brief quotations embodied in critical articles or reviews – without the written permission of the author.

Copyright © 2017 by Harold Stromberger

Registration Pending

# DEDICATION

This book would still be languishing in my C-Drive had it not been for the collaborative effort of many individuals who took the time and had the patience to proofread my story. Thanks to their input and encouragement throughout the years the story stayed alive. As I relocated I would join different writers' groups; their collective efforts helped me fine tune the story.

# To Chase a Ghost

| | | |
|---|---|---|
| 1 | It's Friday of Memorial Day Weekend 2001 | 1 |
| 2 | Charles Picks up Mr. Burton | 6 |
| 3 | Arrival at Meigs Field and Meeting with CEO | 10 |
| 4 | Burton Files Flight Plan | 15 |
| 5 | Burton Departs from Meigs for Benton Harbor, MI | 19 |
| 6 | First Mayday Call | 31 |
| 7 | Second Mayday Call | 37 |
| 8 | Marine 19 Bravo Joins the Search | 42 |
| 9 | Burton Tries to Kill the Engine | 47 |
| 10 | Marine 19 Bravo Chases Down Aurora Air Traffic Lead | 49 |
| 11 | Burton is Found | 53 |
| 12 | Rescued but not out of Danger | 58 |
| 13 | Queen of the Lakes | 64 |
| 14 | The Search for Land | 69 |
| 15 | Chicago Trauma Center | 71 |
| 16 | Doc Confronts Burton | 82 |
| 17 | Saturday of Doc's Party | 87 |
| 18 | Early Sunday Morning | 114 |

| | | |
|---|---|---|
| 19 | Doc and Bill go to the Trauma Center | 120 |
| 20 | Doc and Bill Race to Burton's condo | 123 |
| 21 | United Flight 659 to Seattle | 126 |
| 22 | Doc and Bill Gain Access to Burton's Condo | 128 |
| 23 | Back Onboard Flight 659 | 134 |
| 24 | Back at Mr. Burton's Condo | 140 |
| 25 | Lunch Onboard Flight 659 | 146 |
| 26 | Doc and Bill Arrive at Meigs Field | 155 |
| 27 | Onboard the Grumman Two Hours out of Meigs | 161 |
| 28 | Burton Reaches Seattle and Catches Ferry | 164 |
| 29 | Doc and Bill Finally Have a Destination, Pacific Shores | 169 |
| 30 | Burton on the Upper Deck of the Ferry to Bremerton | 173 |
| 31 | Sheppard Field on the Pacific Coast | 181 |
| 32 | Burton Drives from Bremerton to the Pacific Coast | 185 |
| 33 | Doc and Bill Leave Sheppard Field for Pacific Shores | 188 |
| 34 | Burton Arrives at Pacific Shores | 190 |
| 35 | Doc and Bill Onboard the Medivac | 214 |
| 36 | Pacific Shores Cemetery | 216 |

*Stromberger*

# IT'S FRIDAY OF MEMORIAL DAY WEEKEND 2001

We are in the Gold Coast area of Chicago. So named for the accumulated wealth of the residents and its opulent location along Lake Shore Drive, just north of the Loop. The area is studded with multi storied condos opposite the Lake Michigan beach; this is without question the most expensive and exclusive area within the city proper.

A man dressed in a beige, one-piece flight jumpsuit stands on his balcony 20 stories above the street which gives him an unobstructed view of the beach that runs for miles along Lake Michigan's western shoreline. If today is any indication, the weatherman has fulfilled his promise for outstanding weather for the holiday weekend. The terrific weather has tempted hundreds of people to take off Friday to add an extra day to the holiday weekend.

From his vantage point he observes the invasion of sun worshipers, all sizes and ages, ranging from infants in strollers to the elderly just sitting in their lawn chairs taking in the beginning of what promises to be a magnificent day. The sand is already dotted with beach towels; the bicycle path has the occasional biker or joggers. There's even activity at several of the beach volleyball nets.

He can hear the laughter coming up from the crowd above the sound of the traffic below on Lake Shore Drive. Suddenly, one young voice rings out above the rest. Looking in the general direction, it appears to come from a little girl, perhaps six. She is running through the sand with what appears to be her father and younger brother trying to get a beautiful multicolored kite airborne. She screams with joy, as only little girls can, when the kite suddenly becomes airborne. The spectacular colors of the kite are only further accented by the clear blue sky. He stands for an extra minute with his attention focused on the joy shared by her brother and father over their accomplishment.

The phone rings, but he waits for a few seconds longer to view the family. He walks in from the balcony too late to catch the call. The answering machine kicks in; "This is the Burton residence, I am not able–" he interrupts the machine message, noting that the caller ID display indicates it's from his driver, Charles.

"Good morning Charles."

"Good morning Mr. Burton, I expect to be there in about thirty minutes."

"That's fine; I have a few things to finalize for my flight."

"Very good sir, I will see you soon."

On his way back to the deck the TV catches his attention. The announcer is discussing the possible favorites in the upcoming Indy 500 Race.

"This Sunday will be the 76th running for the Indianapolis 500. Hopefully the 2001 season will be better than last which saw several drivers seriously injured on the Open Wheel racing circuit. Only time will tell if the major design changes in both frame and drivers safety cages promise the drivers more security."

He walks back to the balcony. Unable to locate the family on the beach, he sees the distinctive kite and follows the string back to the father and kids still overjoyed with their success. For a minute a smile comes over his face and then he turns back into the apartment to address some unfinished business before Charles arrives.

His flight bag, flight calculator and aeronautical map covering the Illinois, Indiana and Michigan area are on the dining room table. Earlier this morning he plotted his course with a red pencil for a direct flight from Meigs to Benton Harbor, MI airport, this is his intended flight path, which is entirely over Lake Michigan. Working with a handheld flight calculator, which takes into consideration the effect of the wind on his aircraft and adjusts the land speed accordingly determines his time in flight. By using his adjusted air speed he determines the point-of-no-return. Measuring this distance along his flight path he marks the position with a red "X."

The point-of-no-return is critical knowledge to a pilot whose flight path is entirely over a large body of water like Lake Michigan. Should he experience trouble after passing this point in his flight path, it would be wiser to continue to his destination.

He slowly folds the map and returns it with the calculator to the flight bag; then goes to the bathroom and selects a bottle from the medicine cabinet. Pausing in his bedroom on his on the way back to the dining room he picks up an 8 x 10 picture of an older couple from the top of his dresser and adds it to the flight bag.

Returning to the balcony, he stands for a few seconds watching the people enjoying the beach and one last glimpse of the bright colored kite, now higher than his balcony.

The phone rings, breaking his focus on the beach. The display reads, Lobby Desk. Upon answering the phone he is informed that Charles has arrived.

He picks up his flight bag and stands for a few seconds scanning the condo. On the way out he places an envelope with the name "Maria" written on it in the middle of the kitchen table.

## CHARLES PICKS UP MR. BURTON

Exiting the elevator he is greeted is greeted by the Desk Manager.

"Good morning Mr. Burton, have a great day."

"You also, Dennis."

Charles has pulled the limo up to curb in front of the building and has come around to open the door. Charles greets him; "Good morning Mr. Burton."

"Good morning, Charles."

"The traffic is a little heavy we should be at Meigs in about thirty minutes."

The traffic on Michigan Avenue is congested, stop-and-go at best. They are stopped for a light along the curb. The limo's dark tinted rear windows reflect the covers of the magazines on the news stand on the sidewalk. The business magazine covers have an assortment of pictures of a distinguished looking man in his late 50's/early 60's. The pictures range from head only to full body shots. Collectively they portray a man six foot tall in very good physical condition. His face is handsome yet rugged. The single feature that stands out in every picture is his deep green eyes. The assorted captions read:

"THE MYSTERIOUS ICEMAN REACHES THE PINNACLE", "ICEMAN GETS THE NOD, NOW MAYBE WE WILL FIND OUT WHO HE IS", "THE ICEMAN FREEZES OUT THE COMPETITION AT OMNI", "HERALD THE COMING OF THE ICEMAN", "ICEMAN GETS OMNI GOLDEN RING."

These and an assortment of other statements openly speculate that the Iceman is heir apparent to the CEO's job at OMNI Corporation, a major fortune 500 company. The current CEO, Bill Langman Junior, is stepping down after a recent mild heart attack.

The Iceman has kept his past private. No matter how hard the media have searched all they seem to know is that he is an only child and his parents are deceased. After completing a two year tour in the Army, he worked as a consultant to OMNI before Mr. Longman Senior hired him 25 years ago. His first responsibility was to get a financially failing major division that produced ice for commercial contracts into the black. He not only turned around the division in record time but its profits carried the company through several lean years that followed. This success gained a great deal of notoriety in the business world, thus the nickname "ICEMAN." His marriage ten years ago lasted less than two years. From their marriage through the divorce, even in a recent interview, his ex-wife has always spoken of him with respect and admiration. If there is a kink in his armor, it has escaped detection by the press.

The tinted rear window comes down halfway, clearly revealing the passenger in the back seat. The publications still reflect against the bottom half of the open window. There is no mistake; it is the Iceman inside the limo.

Glancing at him in the rearview mirror, Charles asks, "Did you really get that nickname from saving the Commercial Ice Division?"

A smile accompanies his response, "Yes, I guess I was lucky it wasn't a Gynecology Division."

**Stromberger**

Mr. Burton picks up the phone and dials Mr. Bob Martin, Corporate CFO. "Good morning Bob, I want to thank you again for having Faye's paperwork ready yesterday. I know it was short notice but I wanted to get it taken care of before the holiday weekend.

"No problem, Jack, as per your request, her raise is effective as of this morning. Don't wait too long if you want to surprise her. This kind of news hits the grapevine real fast."

"You're right Bob; I'll see you and Mary at Doc's party tomorrow night."

Mr. Martin seems surprised, "You're going to Benton Harbor and back by tomorrow night?"

"Yeah, it's not that far, I will do an overnight in Benton Harbor and can easily be back in Chicago by noon. It's a chance to build up my cross country miles."

"Have a safe journey Jack, see you tomorrow."

## ARRIVAL AT MEIGS AND MEETING WITH CEO

The drive along Lake Shore Drive to the airport is slow. The normal thirty minute trip takes almost an hour before the maroon limo rolls up in front of the Flight Operation Office at Meigs.

"Here we are, Mr. Burton." Charles asks, "Do you need a pickup upon your return?"

"Thanks, but I have made arrangements, you and your family have a great Memorial Day weekend."

"Thank you Mr. Burton. Have a safe trip; I will pick you up Tuesday at the regular time."

As Mr. Burton walks toward the Flight Operations Office in the base of the Meigs tower he notices the OMNI corporate jet and sees the pilot, Rick Lee. Rick waves and walks over to the fence.

"Good morning, Jack. I better get used to calling you 'Mr. Burton' next week."

"Jack will do just fine, even after next week. Is Mr. Langman here yet?"

"Yes, he is, we leave for Indy right after your meeting."

"Good, we shouldn't be too long. Have a safe flight."

"Where are you headed, Jack?"

"Benton Harbor for a quick cross-country trip."

"After the weekend, you won't have to file flight plans. That will be my job as your corporate pilot. Speaking of that, I better finish my preflight check."

"Take care, Rick."

"You too, Jack."

Mr. Burton starts toward the Flight Operations Office. On his way he pauses for a moment to glance over at the Chicago skyline, a beautiful sight from the airport. The buildings along Michigan Avenue have a variety of heights and sizes, not unlike a set of giant Chess pieces.

Entering the Flight Operations Office he goes to the conference room and is greeted by Mr. Langman, Jr.

"Hi, Jack, or should I call you by your editorial nickname, Iceman?"

"Jack will do fine, sir, what can I do for you?"

"You always ask, 'what can I do for you?' You're one of the few people I know who truly means it. It's about time I did something for you. We have worked together for almost twenty five years. In appreciation for your help and recognition of your accomplishments I recommended you as my successor at the board meeting Wednesday. I don't anticipate any trouble from the Board of Directors; in fact, all the members have long recognized your ability. We decided to make the announcement after the holiday weekend," adding with a chuckle, "It looks like someone leaked the decision."

"Thank you, sir. I would not be here if it wasn't for your confidence in hiring me."

"Hiring you was one of the only decisions my father and I openly disagreed on. I want you to know, we could not have pulled this company together without your help. It is a shame he passed without realizing your potential."

Mr. Burton smiles, "Well, I'm sure glad you did; thanks again."

Jr., with a note of concern in his voice, "However, this promotion comes with one catch."

"What would that be, sir?"

"I am expressing the only reservation some of the board members and I share. I want you to know up front your contract will have a provision that you cannot pilot a private plane while you are CEO. When you accept this position, you have a responsibility to the stockholders to avoid any unnecessary personal risks. I know your passion for piloting; that's why I am asking you to give me your word that you will give up piloting private aircraft." Jr. looks him straight in the eye and asks, "Do I have your word?"

In a reassuring tone Burton says, "Sir, I am flying to Benton Harbor this morning. As much as I love flying, I give you my word that the flight back tomorrow will be my last. I will never pilot a plane while CEO of your company."

"Agreed, I felt this had to be brought up now so you had a chance to consider the situation."

"I appreciate your concern and respect your position."

Half-jokingly Jr. counters, "I suppose there's no chance I could talk you into joining us in Indy and skipping this flight?"

"I just can't quit cold turkey. I really have planned this flight." He then adds in a committed tone, "But I can reassure you my return will be my last flight as a private pilot."

Jr., in a consolatory tone responds, "I had to try, Jack. Well, have a safe flight and a good holiday weekend."

"Thanks for letting me know about the private pilot clause. How long have you been going to the big race?"

"My father first took me when I was seven, been going ever since."

"Well, have a good time, see you on Tuesday."

They shake hands and Mr. Burton walks with Mr. Langman out to the flight line and over to the Corporate jet. They shake hands and Jr. goes up the stairs and waves as he enters the plane. Mr. Burton stands for a few minutes to watch the sleek corporate jet take off and head south.

## **BURTON FILES FLIGHT PLAN**

Burton enters the tower and walks down the hall, entering the door marked, "Pilots Operations Room." This is the area where pilots register their proposed flight plans with the field flight officer. This is a formality that declares their departure time, flight path and expected time of arrival at their final destination. The airport staff has no authority over his flight and cannot make him change his path or destination. They can, however, comment and suggest changes, but the pilot is not bound by their opinion.

Before filing his flight plan he stops at the aircraft rental desk. While signing for the Piper Cherokee rental aircraft, he kids with staff at the desk, "Do you have any sea planes yet?" He knows they don't, but jokingly asks anyway.

The desk attendant replies with a smile, "Not yet, Mr. Burton, but you'll be flying Cherokee 1059Z. It's the third aircraft in the transient parking area. Have a safe flight."

"Thanks, I'll be back tomorrow afternoon."

He then walks down the hall to file his intended flight plan with the Flight Manager. He unfolds his map and describes his course, which is drawn in red on his flight map as it crosses Lake Michigan almost directly east to Benton Harbor, MI.

The operations manager comments, "Your flight path is directly across the lake, not along the shoreline."

Mr. Burton counters with a smile, "I think it's about time I took the big boys' path."

Field Manager Pete Richards happens to be standing at the end of the counter. He knows Mr. Burton, and jokingly quips, "Remember, there are old pilots, and there are bold pilots, but there are no old, bold pilots."

Mr. Burton responds, "I've gone around the shore line at least twice. Should I encounter a problem I am familiar with the location of the alternate airports along the shoreline."

Pete tries to emphasize the problem of single engine failure over an extended body of water, "That's true, but you still have only one engine, unless they added one to the Cherokee last night."

Mr. Burton comments while putting the maps back in his flight bag. "You will hear when I call Chicago radio to close my flight plan at Benton Harbor. Bet I make it without getting wet."

Pete comments apologetically. "As you know, we act in an advisory capacity only. I didn't mean to challenge your piloting capability, just pointing out, should anything go wrong, you will be totally dependent on a single engine and its reliability."

"I understand, and appreciate your advice. Tell me Pete, haven't you flown direct?"

"You know I have," Pete adds, "and it gave me the jitters without land under my craft from take off until landing."

"I am sure I'll have second thoughts about half-way out but I can always opt to come inland and continue along the Indiana shoreline."

"Well, as long as we can't change your mind, have a safe flight. It'll be a little late to turnaround at Benton Harbor tonight."

"You're right, Pete, I'll be staying overnight there and return tomorrow afternoon." Addressing the crew at the desk he adds, "Thanks for your help, and have a great holiday weekend, guys."

## DEPARTURE FROM MEIGS TO BENTON HARBOR, MICHIGAN

Leaving the tower he walks along the flight line to his aircraft 1059Z. It's a beautiful Piper Cherokee painted red-over-white. He sets his flight bag on the wing and takes a few minutes to do a preflight inspection. Upon completing the inspection, he opens the door and enters the cockpit. He positions the flight bag on the passenger's seat for easy access. After securing the five point safety harness he takes the maps out of the bag and adjusts the radio head set. Once settled in he engages the ignition; the engine starts immediately. After a few minutes the engine is warm and he advances the throttle half way. The engine strains against the brakes as he checks the instruments. Everything is ok, so he throttles back the engine to an idle.

At larger airports, he would call Ground Control on one frequency to get taxi instructions and then be passed to Flight Control for clearance to take off. Meigs has a single runway so the tower has a single frequency to handle both taxi and take off instructions. He cuts the throttle back and checks each instrument. Once satisfied, he calls the tower to inform them that he is ready for taxi instructions. "Meigs Tower, this is Cherokee 59 Zulu." (During communications, the aircraft is identified by the aircraft type, the last two numbers of the aircraft number and the alpha letter that follows the numbers; in this case Zulu for Z). "Requesting permission to taxi and hold short of active runway."

The tower operator responds, "59 Zulu, this is Meigs Tower. You are cleared to taxi to the north end of the taxiway and hold for incoming traffic."

"Roger tower." He advances the throttle enough to slowly pull out of the parking area and onto the taxi-way to the north end of the field. He stops clear of the active runway so the inbound aircraft can land. Once the incoming Cessna has landed and cleared the active runway the tower calls him.

"59 Zulu, this is Meigs tower, you are cleared to taxi onto the active runway. After takeoff climb out to 600 feet and turn left to heading zero nine zero degrees and depart air corridor three miles out. Then pick up your flight heading."

This is extremely convenient because the zero-nine-zero, or 90 degrees, heading is directly east and that is almost his exact course on flight plan.

"Tower this is 59 Zulu acknowledging your departure instructions."

"Roger, 59 Zulu, have a safe flight, and keep dry." Meigs is a small airport and word of his direct flight over the lake has already reached the tower crew.

Jack responds with a smile in his voice, "Roger, tower, I certainly intend to."

He slowly taxis to the center of the active runway, positioning the Cherokee on the centerline. The view over the cowl is unusual, the lake surrounds him on both sides, the thin strip of runway ends abruptly at the other end less than 50 feet from the water's edge. You better have enough power to keep airborne when you lift off the runway or Lake Michigan will add one more plane to its scoreboard.

The Cherokee responds as he applies the throttle and the small aircraft charges down the runway, lifting off with ease in less than 1000 feet.

Suddenly, the small runway disappears under the cowl and all he can see is the lake, it's like taking off from an Aircraft Carrier. Continuing south he follows the towers instructions and climbs to 600 feet, then executes a left hand turn as he heads almost directly east over the water on his flight path to Benton Harbor.

The Chicago skyline is now slowly disappearing behind him as the Cherokee continues to push him farther and farther over the water and away from the security of land. According to his flight plan, the next time he will have land under his plane will be on his final approach to the single runway at Benton Harbor Airport. Its runway is 1,000 feet of the opposite shore.

Following flight protocol, once airborne and on his departure course Burton activates his flight plan, "Chicago Radio Center, this is 59 Zulu. I am airborne and clearing your air corridor, please activate my flight plan."

Chicago Radio Center replies, "59 Zulu, this is Chicago radio, your flight plan is activated. Good luck."

"I acknowledge, my flight plan has been activated. Thank you Chicago Radio."

Once that's accomplished he takes time to glance over his shoulder to watch the Chicago skyline for a few minutes; soon only the larger buildings are distinguishable. He returns his attention to the compass to make sure the distraction has not taken him far off course. It only takes a minor adjustment to get back on his heading for Benton Harbor. He then trims out the plane for straight and level unattended flight. The rest of the flight should require nothing more than an occasional check of the instruments and minor adjustments.

He can now turn his attention to other matters as he removes a bottle of pills and the 8 x 10 inch framed picture of his parents that he added in the flight bag before he left his condo. He looks affectionately at his parents, both having passed away years ago. He removes the back of the picture frame and carefully slides out a picture from behind the one of his parents. The second picture is of an attractive young girl standing on a tree stump, high on a hill overlooking a river far below.

She is in her early 20's at most, and her smile radiates the unmistakable glow of a person in love. It's an expression that you can't describe, but recognize immediately if you are fortunate to be the person they are looking at. She is wearing a burnt orange sweater that accents her full bust line and a dark brown straight skirt that falls just below her knees. Her slim figure and white high heels maximizes her 5'8" height. She has blond hair cut short, pixie style, surrounding a lightly tanned face with deep blue eyes that have the promise of passion. Written diagonally across the right hand bottom corner; "Wherever we are Burgie, we will always be together," then underneath, "Love, Margo."

Soon after arriving at Fort Lewis, one of the girls at the USO Club in Tacoma gave him the nickname "Burgie", and it stayed with him throughout his two year tour. He spends the next 15 minutes scanning every detail on the picture. His thoughts go back to the days when he was in the Army.

He was returning from a one-month Thanksgiving leave. Upon reporting for duty he discovered his Battle Group was engaged in a Category 5 Alert. They departed a few hours earlier for a predetermined secure-and-hold area deep in the woods along the Pacific Ocean. In anticipation of his return, a Jeep was waiting to take him to a rendezvous point to catch up with his company. He did not have time to call her before he was whisked off to three arduous days in the woods.

Once back at Fort Lewis, the field gear had to be cleaned and inspected before anyone was allowed outside the restricted area. It only took a few hours but seemed like an eternity. Once dismissed, he rushed to a phone and called St. Joseph's School of nursing in Tacoma.

Reaching the switch board, he asked, "Can I speak with Marguerite?"

*It seemed to take forever for them to find her. She finally got to the phone, "Hello, this is Marguerite."*

*"Hi, Margo, this is Burgie. Hope you had a good Thanksgiving."*

*There was warmth in her voice, mixed with surprise. "Hi, Burgie, it's nice to hear from you. I thought you might have forgotten me. After all, it's been a month."*

*"Are you kidding? In fact, I realized how much I missed you. Would you like to catch a show tomorrow?"*

*"Gee, Burgie, I have a real heavy study load coming into the mid-term exams before Christmas break. I have to keep up my GPA to maintain my scholarships. Would you like to come over later tomorrow evening and we can go for a ride and spend some time together?"*

*"Hey, that's great."*

*"I am trying to get ahead, so I have some time the weekend before*

*Christmas. We have a Christmas Dance at the Tacoma Yacht Club: would you like to take me?"*

*Burgie responded enthusiastically, "You bet I would. That would be great. I will be over tomorrow, say around seven, and we can discuss the dance details, if that's all right with you?"*

*Margo answered with a mixed tone of happiness and conviction. "Sure, I'll need a study break by then, but we can't spend more than an hour or so, do you understand?"*

*"Sure I do, see you tomorrow night."*

He is snapped back to reality when a flash of light catches his eye; it's a reflection of the sun behind him off the wing strut. He hesitates for a moment to check the instrument panel. Then he reaches in the flight bag again and takes out a very old Webcor tape player and a couple of cassettes he packed earlier in the week. By today's standards it is bulky; it was one of the attempts at making tape recorders portable; somewhat like comparing the old "brick" portable phone to the latest generation of cell phones. His condo has the latest home/studio stereo digital system. Yet, on occasion, he plays the older cassette that he has pre-recorded from older phonograph albums that he and Margo enjoyed together.

He recalls his home in southwest suburbs of Chicago. He had worked the summer after his discharge from the Army. He had decided to return to school for the fall semester. His parents were very supportive. They suggested he live at home when enrolled at a local Junior College. He worked as a bartender after school, on evenings and weekends.

As a surprise, he also bought a recorder for Margo and recalls their first phone conversation after he sent it to her in Washington.

>*"Hi, Margo, did the tape recorder arrive intact?"*
>
>*"Yes, Burgie, you shouldn't have spent all that money."*

*"I also got one for me; I figure we can use them in classes to take notes, and mail each other recorded tapes. You know how I hate to write long letters."*

*"Burgie, I will cherish it always. This is the most thoughtful gift I have ever received. I must have listened to the beautiful message you recorded at least a dozen times."* Continuing with a blushing tone in her voice, *"I'm glad no one was with me when I played it. It's real personal, but I sure did like it."* Then, adding with enthusiasm, *"I checked with Mom and Dad of course, and they said it's Ok for me to come to Chicago this Christmas to meet your parents. It was so nice of them to invite me."*

*"Fantastic, please thank your parents for me. I can hardly believe it, last year I'm in the Army and spend Christmas with your family in Pacific Shores and this Christmas you will be with my family in Chicago. I've told my*

*folks so much about you and how thoughtful your parents were that they just had to meet you. I hate to say this, but I better hang up for now. I have to get over to work at the Country Club tonight. Love you, Margo."*

*"I love you, too, Burgie. Remember, wherever we are, we will always be together."*

## FIRST MAYDAY CALL

Burton snaps back to reality when he hears the beginning of a broadcast to all air craft in the area. He does not want to be distracted; all he hears before shutting off the radio is, "Alerting all aircraft in the Michigan City area."

He looks at his watch to determine time in flight since leaving Meigs and enters it into the flight calculator. The calculator determines distance flown; taking into consideration wind direction and air speed. Plotting the result along his flight path he realizes he's crossed the point-of-no-return. He sits for a few minutes staring at the map then confirms his resolve to go forward with his plan.

He turns the radio back on and dials 121.5; the international emergency radio frequency which is continually monitored by all major airports. He starts his transmission, but sporadically pushes the transmit button on the side of the microphone. This will break up his transmission, simulating a possible electrical problem.

*"Mayday, Mayday, Mayday, this is Cherokee 59 Zulu--. I am exper------- electrical*

*prob----. I am past the point of -- --turn. Continuing on to Benton Har---. Do you re-- over?"*

He waits for Meigs to respond to his distress call. "Cherokee 59 Zulu, this is Meigs Field, do you read? Cherokee 59 Zulu, do you read?" He turns off the radio without replying. Even as he sent the message his aircraft is performing without problem!

## PILOT READY ROOM AT MEIGS TOWER

Frustration sets in quickly at Meigs as they continue trying to reach him. They have no way of knowing, nor would they expect he has turned off his radio. They have been able to piece together enough of his message and determined he is having electrical trouble and continuing on to Benton Harbor. They continue calling, with no response.

The Field Manager, Peter Richards, has a speaker in his office that monitors radio traffic so he is already aware of the problem as he bursts into the ready room and blurts out, "God damn private pilots, I warned him not to trust a single engine over water."

Scanning the room for input he adds, "Maybe we can get lucky, someone find out if the Coast Guard has a chopper at Phillips Beach. If they have, it would certainly shorten their time to reach him if he has to ditch."

Assistant Manager Steve Morgan quickly responds, "I'm on it, Pete."

He puts the call on the speaker; it's imperative that they all know what is going on to maximize their opportunity for input as the situation unfolds.

The operator answering the phone barely gets out the words, "This is Phillips Beach Coast Guard Station."

Steve's voice reflects his anxiety, "This is Meigs Field. We have a bird over the lake in trouble; do you have a chopper on site?"

"Yes, we do." A pilot has come up from the ready room and takes the receiver. "Meigs, this is Captain James. We have been monitoring your bird's mayday call. My crew is out on the tarmac warming up the chopper, how can we help?"

"Captain, this is Peter Richards, Field Manager at Meigs. This bird is just past the point of no return on a direct flight from Meigs to Benton Harbor. Our best bet to save time is have you head directly East while we calculate an intercept heading for you. Do you agree?"

"Roger, Meigs tower. We will be lifting off in a minute. My copilot just signaled we are ready. Use our rescue frequency for further communications."

"Thanks Captain, I hope this bird can stay out of the water long enough to make land, but you will be headed his way just in case he can't make it."

A few minutes go by before Captain James voice crackles over the speaker. "Meigs, this is Captain James on Rescue 4. We are airborne heading due east and awaiting your intercept heading."

Everyone has gathered around the chart table as Steve plots the course for Rescue 4 to intercept Mr. Burtons' projected position. He calls out from the chart, "Pete, give them one one three, but it sure is a long way, according to the calculations. The earliest time to the intercept point is at least 30 to 40 minutes, if he goes down now."

"Thanks, Steve," Pete turns to the speaker phone, "Rescue 4; this is Meigs, did you copy?"

"We copy, Meigs, we will pick up an intercept heading one one three."

"Good luck, Captain, and thanks again for your help."

"Roger, Meigs, we'll keep you informed, Rescue 4, out."

Pete clicks off the phone; "Is there anything we overlooked? Does anyone have any ideas?"

After a pause without any suggestions, Pete adds, "Didn't we have a traffic alert for a Marine maneuver off Sunset Dune near Michigan City?"

Steve, "You're right. That's a hell of a lot closer than Rescue 4 just starting from Phillips Beach. I'll check to see if there was any contact phone number with that alert."

The staff is mulling over any options when Pete returns a few minutes later, "Found the contact number for the Marine maneuver. I have the Commander, General Gavin, on extension 12. I hope some of those Marine choppers are still around."

"Me too, Steve. Would you check Burton's emergency notification file just in case this goes sour? Did you say 12?"

"That's right."

Pete picks up the phone and pushes extension 12, "General Gavin, this is Pete Richards Field Manager at Meigs. We would appreciate some help…"

## **SECOND MAYDAY CALL**

It's about twenty minutes after his first Mayday. Using a compass, Burton draws a line straight north, 90 degrees from his current heading which takes him away from the closest land mass. He banks the Cherokee in a gradual left turn until he picks up the new heading, 010 - straight North. He has deliberately changed his course to one that takes him away from any projected rescue path.

Once on the new course, he turns on the radio and repeats the mayday call again sporadically pushing on the transmission button to simulate an electrical transmission problem. As before the chopped transmission is just clear enough to be sure they know it is him. This time he adds a since of urgency in his tone:

"*Mayday, Mayday, Mayday, to anyone monit—ing this frequency. Th-- -s 59 Zulu out- of Mei-- Fie--. on head--- 110 to Ben--- --rbor. I estimate my posi---- to be past the po—of –no return. My electrical prob--- has worsened. Do not antic----- making Beton -arbor. I rep---t I do not --*

*ticipate making-- -enton Har---. Please resp---- if you read me!"*

Again, he turns off the radio as soon as he hears Meigs trying to respond to his call. Even as he sent the message, the engine is still running perfectly, taking him 90 degrees away from the flight path he reported. It is obvious he has no intention of being found.

He then directs his attention back to the picture of Margo looking at her longingly and murmurs softly, "Soon." He starts to remember that day he took the picture and all the fun they had for the few brief months they shared.

*The picture was taken at Point Defiance Park in Tacoma, Washington. He was stationed at Fort Lewis just outside Tacoma. It was an extremely clear day – the kind that made up for all the dreary ones. The sun highlighted the beauty of the forest and Puget Sound far below and further punctuated how attractive she truly was.*

*That morning he had picked her up at the St. Joseph's School of Nursing in Tacoma. One of his Army buddies worked part time at Scotties Restaurant. He packed enough shrimp in the carry-out box to feed four people, while charging them for only a single lunch. There were a couple different restaurants they favored, and they all had one thing in common: they were extremely reasonable.*

*They drove to Point Defiance, just outside Tacoma and enjoyed lunch on a picnic table alongside Puget Sound. He brought his camera and took a few pictures of them at the table. They had two hours before they had to leave for a party later that afternoon.*

*After sharing a few moments of affection, they walked hand-in-hand along one of the many trails. It was during the walk that he spotted the tree stump; it was least 3 feet above the ground on a slope high above the water.*

*He first had to convince her that this was the perfect setting for a picture. Then came the challenge of getting her, dressed in heels and a skirt, up on top of the stump. After he took the picture, getting her down became somewhat of an awkward and sensual encounter, as he slowly slid down with her body pressed tightly against his. With a grin, he insisted he was just being careful not to drop her. For weeks afterwards she would jokingly accuse him of just trying to feel-her-up – but then with a blush add, "Get your camera and let's see if we can find that tree stump."*

*It was difficult to have a good time on an Army private's pay, but they had so much fun on so little money. She never complained and always appreciated whatever they shared. He once said, "Apart, we are terrific – together, we are MAGIC."*

He would gladly barter all the wealth and power he has accumulated over the years just to experience a few brief moments of that kind of happiness again. He pours a fresh cup of coffee from the thermos and places it on the dash. Glancing again at Margo's picture, he removes the cap from the pill bottle and pours its contents into his palm. He takes a moment to contemplate his next move, and then ingests all but one or two of the pills that slip down the front of his flight suit to the floor then drinks the coffee as a chaser.

## **MARINE 19 BRAVO JOINS THE SEARCH**

Major Bennet, pilot of Marine 19 Bravo, is alone in the cockpit. His copilot, Lt. Bronze, is in back talking with the crew. Normally there would be two enlisted personnel in the back to run the large drop door and winches but this war game was mostly over water so they have two frogmen and a corpsman on board in case of emergencies. Major Bennet has just finished talking to Headquarters and calls to Lt. Bronze, motioning for him to come up to the cockpit.

"Lieutenant, General Gavin has changed our mission; I just got orders to break off from the maneuvers."

"Sounds good to me Major, we can get an early start on the weekend."

"Not really, I want you to look up Meigs Field frequency and contact them. We're supposed to see if we can help out with some kind of emergency involving a private pilot. It must be pretty important if he wants us to break off the maneuvers."

Lt. Bronze gets Meigs on the radio. "Meigs Field, this is Marine Helo 19 Bravo on maneuvers off Michigan City, Indiana, do you read?"

Pete responds, "This is Pete Richards, Field Manager, at Meigs."

"Mr. Richards, we have been ordered to see if we can be of assistance with an emergency with one of your pilots."

"We have a mayday from a civilian aircraft we believe to be in your area; he is on a straight route from Meigs to Benton Harbor and apparently past the point-of-no-return. He is having communication problems but from his last garbled message it appears he is in doubt of making landfall. For all we know he could be in the lake by now. His last reported heading was 083, approximately 25 to 30 miles directly west of Benton Harbor. A Coast Guard helo from Phillips Beach just started after him. You are the closest rescue craft to his location. Can you search that area?"

Bennet responds, "Miegs, this is Major Bennet. We acknowledge your situation and are in that general area, please stand by let me check our fuel status."

Turning to Bronze, "Lieutenant, calculate our intercept course and let's hope the pilot knows where the hell he is." Glancing at the fuel and reserve gages he adds, "Be sure to take into consideration our fuel limitations, we've been up some time."

While Lieutenant Bronze calculates an intercept course Major Bennet calls the crew forward to discuss the change in mission. The helicopter crew has practiced rescues at sea; this may be their first chance to try one for real. The frogmen have done this before and are up to the task.

Lt. Bronze states, "Major, we have more than enough fuel for a look-see. My main concern is that there is not much room for error, since the entire time we will be over Lake Michigan."

"Thanks Lieutenant."

Bennet contacts Meigs. "Meigs, this is Marine 19 Bravo, do you read?"

"This is Pete Richards at Meigs, we read you, 19 Bravo."

"We have enough fuel for a look-see, and are plotting his location and intercept point based on your information; sure hope your projected position for the plane is right, for his sake."

"Thanks, Major. The aircraft is a red over white single engine Cherokee, number 1059 Zulu".

Bennet repeats the information as Bronze writes it down. Red over white, single engine, Cherokee1059 Zulu, correct?"

"Roger, and good hunting, Major."

"Thanks, Meigs, we will keep you informed of our progress."

After ending the communication, Bennet comments, "Direct from Meigs to Benton Harbor in a single engine, what the hell is wrong with the pilot?"

Bronze suggests, "He must be in a hurry. I figure a northeast course with an intercept heading of 020 degrees, with contact in about 20 minutes."

"In a hurry to his grave, 020 degrees it is. Alert the crew to start looking for the plane, or wreckage, it could be anywhere along our path."

The big Sea Stallion lumbers through a quarter circle and picks up the new heading. They sight a private plane about 12 minutes out but the markings are not correct. After what seems forever, they arrive at the intercept point.

Bronze spots another plane off to the east toward Benton Harbor, "Light aircraft on our starboard."

"I see him." Bennet swings the big Sea Stallion to the east and starts to chase it down. As they close the gap, Bronze, looking through the binoculars, calls, "Wrong target, Major, the craft has two engines."

Bennet calls back to the crew as he starts to make a large circle back to the intercept point; "Heads up, guys, I'm going to start making progressively larger circles around the intercept point." Everyone is straining to catch a glimpse of something, even wreckage.

Bennet, "For all we know, without a radio this guy could have come inland and landed already while we're out here flying in circles."

## **BURTON TRIES TO KILL THE ENGINE**

Burton has focused his attention on the picture after making the turn that took him away from the rescue path. He hasn't noticed that the pills have already brought on a numbing sensation.

An affectionate, yet resolute, smile comes across his face as he takes a final look at the inscription "Wherever we are we will always be together," and mutters, "Soon." He slides the picture against his chest and zips up his flight suit, almost as an attempt to somehow protect her from the coming crash.

He starts to reach for the throttle in an attempt to shut off the engine. His arm feels like it has been weighted down. The pills have acted much quicker than he expected. He manages to grab the throttle and struggles to find the energy to cut off the fuel, but manages to push it only half way in before his arm falls limp to his side.

Now semi-conscious with his vision beginning to blur, he makes one last effort to cut the engine.

All he can manage is a wild swing that barely hits the throttle.

The shiny red and white Cherokee is capable of level flight without pilot intervention. However, the partially closed throttle has left only enough power to start a gradual descent toward an unavoidable meeting with Lake Michigan.

# **MARINE 19 BRAVO CHASES DOWN AURORA AIR TRAFFIC LEAD**

Major Bennet picks up the microphone and calls out, "Meigs, this is Marine 19 Bravo do you read?"

Almost immediately Pete responds, "19 Bravo, we read you."

"We have broadened our search from the anticipated intercept point and cannot see a thing. We checked out two private aircraft without luck."

Pete replies. "Aurora traffic has been following the situation and called while you were on your search. After checking their traffic logs history for the general airspace they discovered a plane on the Benton Harbor course that suddenly swung due north about 18 minutes ago. He dropped below radar contact after changing his heading. We figure he is about 18 to 25 miles straight north from you. It's a long shot but it might be him."

Bennet says, "That's a real long shot, Meigs."

"We figure he may have panicked with the electrical problem and got mixed up. Is there any chance you can check out this target? We have a Coast Guard chopper from Phillip's on the way to your area, but he's at least forty minutes away".

"Meigs, give us a minute, I want to get an exact check on our fuel situation. What you're suggesting takes us out even further away from land."

"Standing by."

"Lieutenant, I need an exact fuel onboard status."

Bennet then calls the crew forward from their observation places in the back. "Here's the latest. Meigs wants us to chase down a plane that has changed course due north. It is possible the pilot panicked or the electrical problem has affected his instruments. Bear in mind, we aren't even sure this is the plane; for all we know he could be in the lake by now. The only thing we know for sure is if he is down, it would be dark before anyone else can get to him."

Turning to the frogmen, "What are his chances if he goes down?"

The senior frogman replies, "Major, I know what this lake is like at night; he won't have a chance, especially if he goes down in the dark."

Bennet turns to Bronze, "How's it look?"

"It looks like we have enough to take a quick look-see and then we start on our reserve tanks. It's doable but dicey at best."

"Meigs, this is 19 Bravo, we are going to take a quick look. I will pursue the plane headed north until our fuel situation dictates that we head back for shore."

"Roger, 19 Bravo. Good hunting."

After ending the communication Bennet comments, "Christ, now we're chasing down possible targets that disappeared off a radar screen. We could all end up in a life raft tonight."

Turning the sea stallion north he tells the crew, "OK, everyone, back to your observation stations, let's find this guy. Look for wreckage he could be anywhere along our path."

There is very little conversation for the next few minutes. Everyone is focused on the lake below. The fuel situation is also taking its emotional toll; especially on Bennet and Bronze.

Suddenly, a cry comes from the Crew Chief, "Small aircraft ahead, low to the water off to the starboard"!

Bennet confirms, "I see it, it's about four miles away, low to the water."

Barely visible, but there it is, a single engine craft heading north. They almost missed him because he is so low and in the suns glare. The only question on everyone's mind, is it the right plane?

Lt. Bronze grabs the binoculars and, for a few seconds, that seem much longer, focuses on the numbers on the side of the plane. Straining to read the markings, Bronze finally makes identification, calling out: "59 Zulu -- That's him!"

The crew gives out a cheer. Bennet starts to drop down and applies full power to close the distance. All attention is focused on 59 Zulu and getting the pilot to safety.

# BURTON IS FOUND

## ABOARD MARINE 19 BRAVO

Bennet, "Meigs tower, this is 19 Bravo."

Pete, "This is Meigs, go ahead 19 Bravo."

"We have 59 Zulu in sight and closing; should be alongside in four to five minutes. He cannot see us. We are coming up from above and behind."

## MEIGS TOWER

The speakers are still on in the flight room, a spontaneous cheer erupts. The good news quickly spreads through the tower. The celebration is short-lived when they hear another report about a few minutes later.

## ABOARD MARINE 19 BRAVO

"Meigs, this is 19 Bravo. We have closed in on the plane; it appears to be in a gradual descent. It can't be more than 30 to 40 feet off the water. I am coming along side now. Christ! The pilot is slumped forward in his seat and appears to be unconscious! The shoulder and lap belts are the only thing keeping him up. At this rate of descent, I anticipate he will hit the water in just a few minutes, at the most. I am backing off so we don't get caught up in the impact. We will follow him down. With luck, the plane will stay afloat long enough for the frogmen to get him out. We are going to be real busy for a while so I won't call again until he is down."

Bennet turns his attention to the back and hollers, "Frogmen, listen up. The pilot is unconscious, so work fast. I will have to come in hot after he touches down, so wait for my signal. I'm going to have to put you guys real close."

Bennet turns to Lt. Bronze. "This was supposed to be an electrical problem. It appears the engine is running but at reduced power; at least that is my thought. You agree?"

"I agree, but I am more concerned about getting him out after impact. What do you think his chances are?"

"His landing gear is retracted so the bottom is smooth. If he skips over the water like a flat stone at least the plane will hold together. If the nose goes in the water first the engine compartment will fill and probably pull the plane down before our team even gets into the water." Bennet calls back to the frogmen, "He can't be more than 8 feet above the water, stand by."

The shiny red and white Cherokee slowly settles closer and closer to the water. The propeller tips touch first making large splashes as each blade comes around to hit the surface. Continuing to descend the plane tips slightly forward as the blades start to bend from the impact of going deeper and deeper as the plane settles."

Bennet shouts to the frogmen, "He's about to make contact!"

The plane flattens out just before the body encounters the surface.

Bronze, "He's touching down. Look at that rooster tail!"

The front edges of the wings on each side of the body make first contact with the water. At this speed. the water streams over the top, forming a gigantic plume 15 to 20 feet tall on each side of the craft, trailing along the path of contact. From the wings back the body disappears in the giant sprays trailing the wings. It looks like two giant fingers of a hand reaching up from the lake clinging tenaciously to its prey. The forward motion and energy quickly surrenders to the tremendous drag of the water bringing the craft to a complete halt in about 600 feet.

Bennet, "Fantastic, the plane is intact and afloat." He shouts back, "Frogman team at the door and ready!"

Bennet carefully brings the big chopper to within a few feet behind the wing next to the cabin. "Steady, we want to get close – ready – deploy now!"

As soon as the team deploys Bennet moves forward to a point about 300 feet in front of the plane to keep the prop wash and spray from obstructing the rescue efforts. As the chopper turns around the crew can see that both frogmen are already up on the wing and at the cabin door.

# **RESCUED BUT NOT OUT OF DANGER**

The plane has already sunk to the point where the wings are just under the surface. The frogmen find the door has not jammed shut from the impact. In fact, from the choppers view, except for the bent tail and propeller blades the plane looks like someone just placed it on top of the water.

As the rescue team opens the door water gushes into the cockpit, the flight bag, maps and the pill bottle are washed off the seat. It doesn't help that the pilot sits on the left side and the door is on the right side.

The senior frogman ethers the cockpit and instructs his partner to wait at the door. There isn't enough room in the cockpit for both of them to effectively carry out their mission. In addition to the fast rising water in the small compartment the frogman has to struggle with an unconscious pilot leaning forward in a five-point safety harness. Ironically, the harness the helped save the pilots life is becoming a major determent to his rescue.

The water rapidly rises to chest high in the cockpit, causing the plane to list away from the door making the task of pulling the unconscious pilot out even more difficult. The frogman finally gets Burton out of the harness. Burton is a tall man and his unconscious state makes it extremely difficult to maneuver him toward the door through the incoming water. Suddenly, the plane starts to roll over. A surge of water pins both the frogman and Burton against the far wall. The frogman on the wing reaches in and grabs Burton's right arm just as the last gush fills the cockpit, causing a turbulence and backwash that allows him to pull Burton out of plane. The plane continues to roll and plunges, nose first, under the water.

Bennet asks, "They got the pilot, where is the second frogman?"

All that is left above the water is the red tail section, which disappears quickly. After a few anxious seconds, Bronze points, "Over there, on the other side, thirty or so feet away, the second frogman just bobbed up on the surface."

Bennet, "Let's get back in and pull them out, they must be exhausted." He shouts to the crew in back, "Heads up, they're out. We're starting back in. Lieutenant you better go back and see if you can help."

The big chopper lumbers back, the men in the water are almost lost in the spray off its big blades. Bennet has to depend on the Crew Chief for final approach directions. The Crew Chief brings him just over the trio in the water. The frogmen slide Burton into the lowered rescue basket. One frogman makes the trip up to the door with him to insure he doesn't fall out. The corpsman immediately starts to evaluate Burton's condition as the second frogman is being lifted to the safety of the big chopper. The shiny red and white Cherokee has been claimed as another prize by Lake Michigan, but they have saved the pilot.

Bronze returns to the front and brings Bennet up to date. "Major, the frogmen are exhausted, but not hurt. The pilot is still unconscious, except for a gash on his forehead; he appears to be in relatively good shape."

"Lucky bastard, I'll bet he'll have some sore shoulders and ribs from the harnesses."

The corpsman is attending to Burton, and the excitement of the rescue is starting to subside. Suddenly, the "low fuel" alarm flashes betting Bennet's undivided attention. The alarm is triggered automatically when they start to use their reserve tanks. Bronze hits the by-pass switch and does a quick check of their fuel, confirming the situation they both feared.

"Major, the extended rescue has not only consumed more fuel than anticipated, but has taken us further from Indiana. According to my calculations, Indiana is now too far away; we only have enough fuel to reach the Michigan coast, and that's a stretch."

The corpsman calls forward, "Major, the pilot is almost comatose; his vital signs are worsening."

Bennet picks up the handset. "Meigs Field, this is 19 Bravo. We have the pilot on board. He is unconscious, but alive; he has taken a beating from the crash, but my corpsman said nothing appears to be broken. However, he is not responding and seems almost comatose and his vitals are worsening. If that isn't enough, we also have a critical fuel situation."

Pete, "There's a Trauma Center in Michigan City."

"Not possible, we don't have enough fuel to reach Indiana. We are heading east to Michigan; that's the closest shoreline to our position."

## MEIGS TOWER

The initial celebration a few minutes ago in the ready room is quickly replaced by silence as the transmission continues over the speaker.

"19 Bravo, the best chance for the pilot's survival is to get him to a Trauma Center, are you closer to Chicago? Is there any way you can stretch your–".

Bennet cuts him off, "Chicago is out of the question. We are headed for the closest coast line, which is Michigan." Adding, "And that is in question."

"19 Bravo, the Coast Guard chopper, Rescue 4, should be at your location in ten to fifteen minutes at most."

"Meigs, we can't wait, and I don't want to risk leaving the pilot in a raft to wait for pickup. If you don't have any other suggestions, we better keep going toward Michigan, do you agree?"

Pete reluctantly replies, "Agreed, let us know where you anticipate landfall, so we can dispatch an ambulance to meet you at the beach."

"Will do, 19 Bravo out."

## QUEEN OF THE LAKES

*Queen of the Lakes* is one of the large freighters traveling up and down Lake Michigan delivering iron ore to the steel mills. Her radio operator has been following the search and rescue operation situation since before the Marine chopper flew past them a few minutes ago.

The ship's captain calls, "Marine 19 Bravo, this is Capt. Liggett, Captain of the ore freighter *Queen of the Lakes*."

Bennet replies; "This is Marine 19 Bravo."

"We are just behind you and off to the southeast. We have been monitoring your radio traffic and may be of help. I have a very large deck with flat cargo hold covers. They cannot support your craft, but you can lower the pilot to us and he can wait for transfer to the Chicago Coast Guard chopper to take him to the Chicago Trauma Center."

"Captain Liggett, this is Major Bennet. Are you sure of your location? We can't go back too far. I'm not even sure we can make land now, without any additional delays."

"Major you passed off our starboard less than five minutes ago. If needed, my navigator will give you an exact heading to us."

There is a short delay, which seems like an hour, while Bennet and Bronze review the options before they respond.

Bennet finally breaks the silence, "Captain Liggett, we will take you up on your offer. We won't need the heading; our crew chief just told me he can see you."

Bennet makes another call, "This is 19 Bravo to Coast Guard Rescue 4, do you read me?"

"Marine 19 Bravo, this is Lt. Brewer in Rescue 4, we have been monitoring your radio traffic."

"Lieutenant, my corpsman is concerned about the pilot's condition. He wants us to leave him with the pilot on the freighter for your pickup. Do you have enough room for both of them?"

"We have room Major, and would welcome his medical help on the trip back to Chicago, over."

Earlier in the day, as the events started to transpire, Pete had Steve check Burton's in-case-of-emergency contact list. Doc was the only one listed,

### Stromberger

so Steve called him and explained the situation. He immediately left home and arrived about an hour ago and has been in the pilot's ready room with Pete's staff, monitoring the communications during the rescue.

Doc turns to Pete, "I can assure the corpsman that OMNI will transport the corpsman him home tonight if he stays with Mr. Burton. Do you want to tell him?"

"Good idea, Doc." Pete picks up the handset and waits for a break in the communications between Captain Liggett and Major Bennet. There is a lull and Pete interjects, "Bravo 19, this is Pete at Megs tower, do you read?"

"Affirmative Meigs."

"Major, we have a representative from OMNI here and he guarantees your corpsman will get home tonight if he stays with Mr. Burton through the transfer."

Bennet responds with surprise, "Burton! Are you telling us we have the Iceman on board?"

Pete responds, "Affirmative, 19 Bravo. Their company doctor will be meeting Rescue 4 at the Chicago Trauma Center."

Bennet calls back to the crew, "Hey, guys, we have the Iceman on board. Frogmen, come on up, I want to talk with you."

The frogmen are slow to respond, clearly revealing their exhaustion from the ordeal.

"First, I want to thank you for one hell of a rescue. I also want you to consider jumping off on the freighter. You are both exhausted and I wouldn't want to put you through another ditch if we run out of fuel. It could get tough and you may not have enough energy left."

The senior frogman immediately responds, "Major, we would be more help here than on a freighter if you have to ditch."

The second adds, "That goes for me too sir."

"Thanks guys, we may need your help."

By this time the big Sea Stallion is approaching the freighter. Bennet turns his attention back to the tricky business of hovering one or two feet over the pitching deck of an extremely large ship in the fading evening light. He cannot touch down because the ship's cargo hold covers cannot support the weight of the helicopter, and they don't have enough fuel for the time it would take to lower the pilot on the winch.

Bennet calls the ship, "*Queen of the Lakes*, this is 19 Bravo. I will be hovering mid-ships over your fourth cargo hold cover. Are there any obstructions that would cause us any trouble?"

"19 Bravo, this is Captain Liggett, you have a clear deck. I have four men on deck to assist in the transfer."

"Thank you Captain, I'll start the transfer within a minute or two. As you know, I don't have time to stay around, so we will pull off as soon as transfer is completed, thanks again."

Bennet maneuvers the big Marine chopper until it settles to within a foot or two above the hold cover. The ship's crew rushes over to retrieve Burton's stretcher from the chopper. The corpsman jumps out onto the deck and accompanies the stretcher to a safe distance from the chopper, taking his attention from his patient only long enough to give Bennet a thumbs up."

## THE SEARCH FOR LAND

The big chopper rises slowly, making sure they have a clear path away from the ship, then tips forward and picks up speed on its easterly direction toward the closest beach along the Michigan shoreline. As soon as they pick up their heading to Michigan Bronze asks, "Are you a betting man, Major?"

"I play seven-card draw Lieutenant; but I don't like my hole cards right now."

"Guess we can't just forfeit the ante."

"Maybe we can draw into a good hand." Laughing, Bennet adds, "According to the computer we either make the beach or we'll be close enough to swim in. Personally, I hope we make the beach. I can't swim worth a damn."

Bennet and Bronze can hear the Coast Guard chopper instructing the freighter to transmit a radio frequency for one minute so they can get an exact fix on their location. Bennet turns his attention forward as he and Bronze search the dim evening light for a glimpse of land.

A little later they monitor the transfer of Burton and the corpsman to Coast Guard Rescue 4 and their start for Chicago and the Trauma Center.

The only activity on 19 Bravo is their final preparation for ditch procedures. Once finalized, the activity is replaced by an eerie silence; they all know that within a few minutes they will be out of fuel and have to ditch if they haven't made landfall.

This is the same lake that not that long ago gave them cause for concern for the survival for a downed pilot. The only difference is that conditions have worsened by the oncoming darkness, and no one is on the way to pick them up if they don't make shore.

It appears that Lake Michigan now is focusing on a new prey.

## THE CHICAGO TRAUMA CENTER

It's almost midnight at the Chicago Trauma Center. Burton was brought in by Coast Guard Rescue 4 over an hour ago. Doc has been sitting in the ER waiting room the whole time. His only news came half an hour ago, when the ER Physician, Dr. Lynch, sent a nurse out to reassure him Jack was in stable condition.

The Navy corpsman steps out of an office after an interview with Dr. Lynch's staff. He is greeted by Doc, "Hi, I'm Doctor Bromes, Mr. Burton's doctor. First, I want to let you know that your chopper and crew made it safely to the beach in Michigan. We sent a tank truck to refuel them and they should be back at your base by now.

The Corpsman replies, "That's great. I felt like I deserted them, but our patient couldn't be left alone on *Queen of the Lakes* to wait for Rescue 4."

"I speak as a personal friend of Mr. Burton, and for our company, when I tell you we all appreciate the rescue and personal risk your team took to get him here."

"Sir, we were lucky to find him at all. He was off course and headed in the wrong direction, it was a miracle Aurora Radar happened to notice him."

"We certainly want to thank you all. There will be a limo here in about ten minutes to take you back to your home. We will be contacting your crew in a few days to extend an invitation for you and your wives to come downtown and be our guests for a weekend."

"You don't have to do that. We would have done the same thing for anyone."

"I know, and that's all the more reason for us to have you come to town on us. Let's walk down to the lobby. The limo should be arriving soon, and I would like to ask you some questions, if you don't mind."

"Yes, sir, but I wasn't allowed in the ER during treatment. I was interviewed in a separate office by the ER staff." Almost as an afterthought he adds, "By the way, did they give you the picture we found."

"No, no one told me about a picture."

"I found it between his shirt and flight suit when we were working on him in the chopper. You're his doctor, so I should mention that there was a pill bottle in the cabin. The frogman team tried to catch it in the swirling water but failed. I thought it might be important."

"I will have to find out about the picture, but you said there was a pill bottle?"

"Yes, sir, the rescue team said they saw only one, but there may have been others."

"That's funny; I haven't prescribed any medication for him recently. I'll have to check into that and the picture. First, I would like to confirm something. I was told he was unconscious before impact, is that true?"

"Yes, sir, we caught up with his plane and came alongside just minutes before impact. He was definitely slumped forward in his seat, unconscious."

"How was he when you got him into the chopper, did he come around?"

"In fact, he really scared us, he seemed comatose. I was afraid he was going into shock. We had made the switch over on the ore freighter deck and were almost back here in the Coast Guard chopper, just about ten minutes from the trauma center, before he began to respond at all. I'll tell you, we were plenty relieved to see his vital signs finally start to improve."

By now they have walked to the pavilion and are waiting on the driveway when catches a glimpse of the limo turning into the driveway.

"Here's your limo. Don't forget, you guys are going to be our guests. Someone will be calling to finalize the dates and details. Thanks again, have a safe trip home and a good holiday weekend."

Doc stands for a moment watching the limo as it disappears down the pavilion ramp. His thoughts are first on Burton's condition, then the pills and then the picture. He slowly walks back to the lobby to catch the elevator. When it arrives, he selects the floor the staff told him Burton would be sent to after his release from the ER. Exiting on Jack's floor, he walks over to the central medical desk and introduces himself to the staff on duty.

"Good evening, or should I say morning, I'm Dr. Bormes, Mr. Burton's personal Physician. I was told Mr. Burton would be brought up to this floor after his release from ER. I would appreciate any information you have on his current status."

The nurse at the desk first checks the computer monitor then looks up. "He just got out of ER and should be up in a few minutes. You are certainly welcome to wait in his room-1256, or, you can wait in the doctor's lounge. I will let you know if there are any changes."

"Thanks, I will wait in his room. Please tell the attending physician I would like to see him when he gets a chance."

"I will leave a message for Dr. Lynch. She's the attending Physician."

"I would appreciate that. Also, there was mention of a photo."

"Yes, there was a wet photo sent up from the ER. We have placed it on the table in his room under a heat lamp to try and dry it out."

"Thank you. I will check on it, no need to come down."

"I will be down with some fresh coffee. It isn't often we get VIPs on the floor, especially the Iceman. If you need anything we are on extension seven. I would appreciate your leaving an emergency number with us."

"I will take care of that before I leave."

Doc walks down to the private room. He can't wait to see this picture so he immediately goes over to the table. Although it suffered a little water damage, he can still make out an extremely attractive young lady, perhaps 19 or 20 at most! She is standing on a tree stump on the edge of a hill. In the background below you can see a large river. The inscription written diagonally across the bottom right hand corner reads, "Wherever we are. Burgie, we will always be together." Then underneath she wrote "Love, Margo."

Doc is puzzled. He has never seen this girl before. What's more, she looks young enough to be Jacks daughter and he has never heard him referred to as "Burgie." He cannot recall seeing that picture in Jack's office, and he never mentioned a daughter. Doc thinks 'Maybe he has a lover, a YOUNG lover', then immediately dismisses the thought because that just isn't Jack's style. He has too much class and he can have his pick of available women his own age. Doc is concentrating on the picture and is startled when the nurse walks in with his coffee.

"Here's your coffee, Dr. Bormes, fresh and hot. We just heard from the ER, Dr. Lynch is coming up with him. They told her you were here and she said she would like to talk to you before I could convey your request to see her."

Doc spends the ten minutes or so before Mr. Burton is up from the ER studying the picture. He is so distracted with the picture that he is again startled when the staff comes to the door with Mr. Burton on a gurney.

Doc is surprised at Jack's appearance; he certainly looks better than he expected. Sure there are some bruises but the only additional trace of his recent experience is a bandage high on the right side of his forehead covering some stitches. Other than that he looks fine; certainly not what you would expect for surviving a plane crash in Lake Michigan. Another nurse has come from the desk. The two nurses and the attendant that came up from ER slide him off the cart and into the bed. Mr. Burton barely makes a sound and appears only semi-conscious. The nurses are hooking up the monitors and IV when Doctor Lynch walks in.

"Hello, Dr. Bormes, I am Dr. Lynch. I treated Mr. Burton when he came into the ER."

The two shake hands.

Doc, with surprise in his voice asks, "Except for a few stitches on his forehead, he looks great on the outside. Are there any internal injuries?"

"Surprisingly not, of course, he will have some real sore muscles and black and blue bruises from the restraints that apparently protected him upon impact. But, other than that, he has come through the experience remarkably well."

"I am sure his physical condition also helped."

"I am sure it was a contributing factor. I would like to discuss some unusual circumstances. Mr. Burton will be out for a while; I suggest we go to the Doctor's Lounge. I'm sure it will be empty at this hour so we can have some privacy."

She guides Doc down the hall to an empty doctor's lounge. After looking around the lounge to make sure they are alone, Dr. Lynch gestures to Doc to be seated. Joining him, she starts, "I thought we would have more privacy down here while they are setting him up. As his doctor, you may be able to help explain a situation. Has Mr. Burton been depressed, or under a lot of stress lately?"

"Well, he is always under stress, but it has never affected his physical health. He should be the happiest person in our company, considering he will be named CEO soon after the holiday weekend. Why do you ask?"

Dr. Lynch hands him the blood workup printout, commenting, "Here are the preliminary blood workups; tell me what you think?"

"It looks good. Wait; look at these high levels of the antihistamine, diphenhydramine, that's a major ingredient in sleeping pills."

"I wanted to bring this to your attention. We ran an extremely inclusive test trying to explain what was reported by the corpsman as an apparent comatose condition when he was rescued or we never would have found it. Are you aware of any medication problems?"

"No, in fact he hardly ever takes an aspirin. That's what makes these results hard to understand, but that dosage level of sleeping pills would certainly explain why he was unconscious before the crash and appeared comatose to the rescue crew."

"Well, these are the preliminaries, but I wanted to talk to you first. I have requested a second test from another sample using a John Doe not to draw attention. If someone got suspicious over a second test, the next thing you know we are reading it in the papers."

"I certainly appreciate your discretion. It would be hard to explain why it appears he took sleeping pills before piloting a plane across Lake Michigan."

"Bear in mind, these test results are after he was rescued. He probably was overdosed, if this was the concentration left in his blood after heaving up half the lake when he was rescued. I can only imagine the results if the entire amount he ingested had dissolved into his blood stream. There appears to be a serious problem."

"I agree, Doctor, I will have to try and get answers as soon as he is conscious."

"You better wait a day or two. I don't think there is a threat as long as we have him here. He needs rest and therapy to relieve the muscle pain. If you want to talk, he will be coming around in half-an-hour, but please keep it brief."

"Certainly, and thanks again for your discretion on the test."

"No problem, I will be available if you need anything, and our staff is here to help. There goes my pager. I better get back to the ER, talk later."

"Thanks again, Doctor, and have a good holiday weekend."

## **DOC CONFRONTS BURTON**

Doc walks back to the room. He looks in and finds that the staff has Mr. Burton all set up, he is still unconscious. Doc walks over to the picture under the heat lamp on the window sill. He almost forgot it with all the commotion about the blood test. Staring at the picture, he mutters to himself "Maybe you can explain this latest revelation." He can't help but wonder, just who she is and where she fit in his friend's life.

Burton lies motionless for almost an hour before he utters a low groan as he starts to roll over in the bed. Doc moves to the bedside and manipulates the IV tube so he won't get tangled. He waits for a minute while Jack comes around. Jack focuses on him and in a strained voice with a confused tone mutters "Doc?"

"Hi, Jack, bet you feel like hell."

There is no response from his friend, only a look of confusion on his face as he tries to focus his eyes while looking around the room.

"Better bring you up to date. It's late Friday, no, actually early Saturday morning. Thanks to a

Marine helicopter on maneuvers off Michigan City, you have survived a plane crash into Lake Michigan. Those guys went the extra mile to get you; they damn near ran out of fuel. It looks like you really got off lucky. Other than a few stitches on your forehead, no one would believe you were in a plane crash."

Jack slowly reaches along his forehead until he touches the bandage, but still no response. Although groggy, he should be verbally responding by now.

Doc continues, looking for a response. "You're going to feel like your worst hangover. All your muscles must ache from the impact and the strain against the safety belts but it kept you from going through the windscreen."

Jack is conscious and semi-alert, but still not a word. Doc wanted to wait at least a day for the next questions but he needs answers now.

"I know this isn't the time," hesitating for a moment, "but there are two things I have to ask you. I wanted to wait until you were rested, but I have to get some answers. The crew reported you were unconscious prior to the crash and your blood test showed an abnormal concentration of diphenhydramine. This is most often the result of someone overdosing on sleeping pills. I have to know, did you take pills before you took off, or during the flight?"

Jack's quick eye movement confirms he is alert but still no answer. He seems either confused by the question or the fact that it has been detected. He motions for Doc to come closer to the bed. In a low and very strained voice he says.

"Please, Doc, let me get some rest. I will have to get my mind straight. I never expected to be here and now I have to deal with that and other things. Please, I just need rest." Jack slowly turns his head away and closes his eyes. It is clear he does not want to confront the problem, at least not tonight.

Before Doc can catch himself he blurts out. "Well, maybe Margo can tell us what is going on."

As soon as he said it, Doc realized this was certainly not the time to confront a second situation. Jack slowly turns back toward Doc with an expression that is a mixture of anger, pain and sorrow. In all the years he has known Jack he has never seen this kind of emotion. Jack truly had earned the nickname ICEMAN.

Apologetically, Doc says "I am sorry, Jack, I truly am. It was inconsiderate of me to pry, especially now. The comment came from a very concerned friend who would do anything to help. Just say it, and I will do it. I owe you a lot, but I would help more as a friend than one who is indebted to you. Do you understand?"

Jack's expression slowly turns to a smile, almost one of forgiveness. In a voice not much more than a whisper he says: "I know, Doc, I will need help, but right now all I want is to be alone and try to figure out what to do next."

"You better get some rest. See you later today. They have my number. If you need anything, don't hesitate. Do you want me to call this Margo and let her know you are OK? I mean she will be concerned."

Jack shakes his head no. Doc leaves the room and begins to realize his primary concern, the crash, has now been overshadowed by the revelations of the blood test and this person Margo.

He checks with the staff at the floor desk then proceeds to his car, almost alone at the late hour in the parking lot. During the ride home he wonders, 'Jack has no immediate family, but here is a man about to take the top rung on the corporate ladder with his face on every prominent business magazine and the only person listed to contact in an emergency is the company doctor. He has isolated himself all these years in his quest to the top'.

Jack had been married, if only for a few months. His ex-wife Carol was the only one from outside the company to call the hospital after the news broke about the crash. She has since remarried and yet she still has concern for him.

Doc begins to wonder, 'Has Margo heard of the accident, or does she even live in Chicago? After all, the picture had heavy trees and a large river, maybe Wisconsin or Michigan. Who can she contact to know how he is doing? Does she care'? He had asked if he should contact her and Jack said no. All the way home he finds himself preoccupied with thoughts about Margo, a person whom he has never met and didn't know existed a few hours ago.

Where does she fit, or does she, in the near death of a friend'?

Finally, he arrives at home, being as quiet as possible getting in the house and upstairs. He manages to change and quietly slip into bed. If he wakes his wife, Pat, she will keep at him for hours prying out all the details. For a moment he shares the Iceman's exhaustion, and then he falls into a deep sleep.

He has left a note for Pat on her dresser, "PLEASE, DON'T WAKE ME UNTIL NOON."

## SATURDAY OF DOC'S PARTY

Pat has been up for hours and more anxious every minute to find out about Jack's condition, but, per his request, she lets Doc sleep until noon. The party doesn't start until 6:00, and it's mostly catered so she let Doc off the hook. She awakens him promptly at noon, then interrogates him for an hour about their friend's condition. He brings her up to date on the events of the previous night; careful to omit the sleeping pills and Margo.

Doc goes over to the hospital around 3:00 to check up on Jack. Except for the bandage on his forehead, Jack looks good. He did acknowledge that he was sore all over, but apparently nothing is broken. He reassures Doc that he appreciates his offer to help, but he will take care of a few issues as soon as he recovered. Jack is quick, almost curt, to add that he will personally take care of the Margo issue. It was apparent he does not want to discuss that or the drugs found in his system after the crash landing.

The visit ends prematurely when a nurse came in to take Jack to therapy. Before leaving, he wishes Doc and Pat a great holiday weekend and expressed his regrets for missing the party later that evening and sakes him to reassure everyone he is all right.

Doc leaves as Jack is wheeled off the therapy. During the drive home he remembers the corpsman's comment at the trauma center, how it was a miracle that they found Jack at all. He was way off course, actually headed north. Then he remembers when he first arrived at Meigs, Pete Richards told him that Jack had an electrical problem before the incident. Doc thinks to himself, *Maybe the electrical problem affected his compass, who knows?* Doc dwells on that comment for a few moments and thinks, *That's not what you would expect from Jack; he was a perfectionist* – maybe it was the drugs in his system that caused him to be disoriented. Either way, it sure was lucky that they were able to find Jack in time.

Jack was more than a social friend. Doc and Pat were indebted to him. He supported Doc when things got rough several years ago after Doc's father passed away. Doc's inheritance was very substantial; the instant wealth took its toll. He started drinking to the point it became a concern to the company. He was about to be dismissed when Jack took his side, a less than popular move, with senior corporate management. His outspoken support was the pivotal reason that kept Doc in the company. He kept his promise to Jack and entered an alcohol rehab program. Within a year, Doc was clean and sober and has stayed that way ever since. That was quite a few years ago but he has never forgotten Jack's help.

After his father passed away, Doc's mother was left alone in her gigantic home. She convinced Doc and Pat to move in with her. She was gone all the time on social trips to visit friends. When home she felt lonesome in the large house. In fact, she was now on a cruise to Alaska and planned to spend at least a month afterward visiting friends out West.

Once Doc got home he brings Pat up to date on Jack's condition; again omitting Margo and the pills. She is relieved to hear their friend has been so fortunate.

## THE MEMORIAL DAY PARTY

Doc's Memorial Day party is second only to the corporate Christmas party. Doc and Pat enjoy entertaining and have several parties throughout the year, but this one is by far their biggest and best effort. They hold it on Saturday as not to interfere with anyone who wants to make the Indianapolis race on Sunday.

The party started around 6:30 and at one point there were at least 100 people. Throughout the evening Doc was the consummate host, attending to everyone and making sure they were having a good time. It wasn't until after 9:00 that Doc finally had a chance to relax. At that point the crowd had thinned to 50 or so guests, clustered in small groups throughout the house, around the pool, patio, and garden area.

Doc was standing by the pool when Bill Hawk, VP of Corporate Security and a close friend over the years, happens to stroll by.

"Hi, Bill, having a good time?"

"Sure am, Doc. You and Pat seem to outdo yourselves every year, how's Jack doing?"

"I stopped in today to check up on his progress. He really came through it well. Sure doesn't look bad considering he survived a plane crash. Lots of sore muscles naturally, but nothing broken. He has a few stitches on his forehead but that's all."

"Hey, that's great! Do you think he'll be able to take over the helm next week?"

"I talked to Mr. Langman earlier today. He called me from Indy to see how Jack was doing and we decided to put off the announcement until Friday, or possibly early the following week. He wants Jack to get some rest so he won't have bruises or stiffness. You know the press; they will be looking for a story, ruthless bastards."

"Doc, that was a miracle having the Marines find him."

"Yeah considering he was headed straight north and miles off course."

"I can't imagine Jack getting lost. Anyway, he sure deserves the top seat. It would be a shame if something happened at the last minute."

"Bill, I would like to talk in private, let's go over to my den." Bill follows with heightened curiosity.

Once inside, Doc closes the door.

Doc starts, "Jack told me he was going to make it a short trip to Benton Harbor to build up his cross country miles and be back in plenty of time for the party."

Bill, "Seems risky, considering he will be our CEO within a few days; you know, Doc, I have him to thank him for my promotion. He really helped me."

"That's one of the qualities that helped him get to the top. He truly deserves the CEO slot." Adding, "That, and the fact he is the last of the nice guys."

"There is something I have to find out, Bill, and you are one of the few people in the company I can trust with this information."

"What is it, Doc?"

Doc asks cautiously. "This may not add up to anything, but have you ever heard Jack mention the name Margo?"

"No, can't say I have. Who is she?"

"That's the question, when Jack was on the Marine helicopter the paramedics started treatment. When they opened his jumpsuit and found an 8-1/2 x 11 picture against his chest."

"They found what?"

"A picture of a lady with an inscription and signed 'Love, Margo'."

"Well, the Iceman has melted. She must be the elusive Lady Luck, considering how things have gone for him the last twenty four hours."

"A *YOUNG* Lady Luck is more like it. My guess is she looks barely twenty."

"Twenty! No wonder he has been acting strange the last two or three weeks, the old pirate. What did he say? 'Eat your heart out'?"

"He had just come around and obviously did not want to talk about it. He was shocked when he heard me mention her name, then he just seemed to withdraw. I told him we would talk about it later and he nodded yes. Today he was very evasive, almost rude, about the situation."

"Do you think she was pushing to come out with his promotion coming up? Maybe they have been dating, she could be pregnant. Wouldn't that be a story?"

"Christ, Bill! I told you I don't know, and I need your help, not your humor."

"Sorry, Doc, we both owe him and this may be our chance to pay up."

"I can't put my finger on it, but after they brought him up from the ER, he seemed more than confused when he came to, but there was something strange in his first response."

"That's easy to explain. I am sure he thought it was all over just before the crash."

"That's part of the puzzle. If there is one, the helicopter crew said he was unconscious when they came up on the plane just before it impacted. The Hospital ruled out heart attack last night."

"Are you telling me that he didn't seem happy he survived?"

"No, he was confused at first and after I explained what happened, he withdrew, something seemed wrong. I can't put my finger on it."

"That sure is hard to explain, but you can count on me if you need any help. Not to worry, though, maybe he will be more open when you talk to him tomorrow. For now, you better get back out there and mingle with the last of your guests."

"Yeah, he won't be released until Tuesday at the earliest. Maybe I am reading too much into the situation."

"Would it be OK if I went with you when you visit him tomorrow?"

"I don't see why not. Maybe you will see something I either missed or misunderstood."

"Great, I'll call around ten and we can catch lunch while we're out."

"Bill, you better get married, you worry too much about eating."

"It's not that, I just hate my cooking. I'm awful at it."

Doc and Bill leave the den laughing; each going their separate ways melding into the partygoers.

All night Doc has been deluged with compliments about the party, immediately followed up with more questions about Jack. Most of them have picked up on the Iceman nickname. While socializing from one guest to another he feels a tap on the shoulder. He turns to see Fay, Jack's secretary.

"Hi, Fay, how's everything going?"

"Having a great time, as usual, Doc. How's Mr. Burton?"

"Doing fine, he will probably be out by Tuesday."

"Doc, you have been friends with him almost from the beginning like me, right?"

"Sure have"

"You're probably one of the closest friends he has in the company."

"I don't know if he is close with anyone, but we are friends; is there any reason you asked?"

Fay looks around. "Can we talk in private later?"

"You look concerned, let's talk now; we can go over by the gazebo. We should have some privacy there."

As they approach the gazebo Doc gestures for her to sit on the bench. She has a worried look on her face. Doc jumps to the conclusion that she is concerned about Jack's recovery and immediately starts to reassure her he is okay.

"Fay, believe me, Jack is all right. All he has to show for the experience is a small bandage on his forehead. He's a bit sore, but he'll recover soon."

"It isn't that, Doc. I know this is not your business, and if you do know you may not want to tell me, but has he mentioned anything about replacing me when he goes to the top?"

Doc is somewhat surprised at her self-serving comment, "He has never said a thing negative about you. He has only praise about your work. What has he said that makes you think he is going to replace you?"

"Something is wrong, Doc. He has been acting strange for almost a month. At first, I thought it was the pending promotion but other things have been happening."

"Give me some examples. It will be between just you and me."

"He's been different, almost secretive, and not easy-going and there was this phone call the other day that really set him off. I've worked with him over twenty years and I have never seen him get so upset. This stranger called and did not want to leave any contact information. Mr. Burton happened to come around the corner and overheard the conversation and told me to pass the call to his office. Just before the door closed I could hear him scream, 'I told you never to call me here!' Ten minutes later he stormed out of his office, telling me to cancel the rest of his day. He has never done that before. He came in the next day real moody. Then there was this incident last Tuesday morning."

"Fay, do you remember if it was a woman on the phone when he got upset?"

"No, it was a man. Why did you ask?"

"Have you ever heard him mention a friend or relative named Margo?"

"No, I haven't, but you know he never discusses his friends, and his parents have been dead for years. His mother died before he started with us and his dad within two or three years after. He is an only child so he has no real family, at least not that I know of."

"You also mentioned something about last Tuesday. Was there another call?"

"No, not another phone call. Actually, there were two incidents that make me suspect he is replacing me. Last Wednesday, before the senior officers; meeting he went out of his way to close his door when he had a meeting with Mr. Martin, the manager of Human Resources. I heard through the grapevine later that Mr. Martin had his secretary personally type some confidential orders.

"It's not just that. I know this sounds crazy, but Thursday, just before he left for vacation, he called me in his office and must have spent 30 minutes telling me how much he appreciated the job I have done over the years. He recalled how we worked as a team to turn the commercial ice division around and how much I have helped him get this promotion. He has always been nice, but he really went to extremes. I might be wrong, but he just seemed to be saying good-bye, almost like he was leaving me behind."

"Fay, he hasn't told me a thing. I will be talking to him tomorrow. If the opportunity comes up, I will find a way to ask him, deal?"

"Thanks Doc. I appreciate your help."

"No problem. I promise I will call tomorrow after I see him."

"Doc, who is this Margo?"

"I have no idea. I hoped you could help."

"Sorry, but thanks again Doc."

"I better get back out to the party and make a few stops to see some more guests before they leave. I will call tomorrow."

Fay and Doc walk back to the party together. Doc starts going from guest to guest. This time he deliberately worked his way toward Bob Martin and his wife Mary. He takes a few minutes to make sure Fay does not notice his course."

"Hi, Bob, Mary, how is your little bundle of joy these days?"

"Funny you should ask: Mary has brought pictures, but they are in the car."

Doc asks, "If you wouldn't mind getting them, I sure would like to see the latest."

Mary counters with a suspicious tone, "I'll go, I know exactly where they are and I think Doc wants to talk to you alone."

"Mary, you are a mind reader, but I do want to see the pictures. After all, I am his godfather. We'll be in the den, the light is better in there."

"Be back in a minute, so you better be fast, Doc."

Doc watches as Mary leaves, then he escorts Bob to the den. "Bob, I know this is not my business, but please indulge me. Is Jack going to replace Fay when he moves to the top? It is important to know, but not for the reasons you may think."

"Well, you can put her mind at ease. Jack even went so far as to push through a raise four months before her review date. In addition, I have heard nothing but praise for Fay. You should have read the performance appraisal to justify the raise he gave her. It took effect yesterday. She would have gotten the raise even if he had not survived the crash. My guess is he wanted to surprise her with the raise next week at his promotion."

"Bob, couldn't that mean he was paying her off as a parting gesture before he would replace her?"

"Doc, I can rule that out. We would have to be interviewing her replacement and we are not doing that. Her logical replacement, Mr. Langman's secretary, has already filled out all the paper work for her retirement, set for when Mr. Langman leaves. So, I don't see it happening."

"Thanks, Bob, I appreciate your confidence in telling me. By the way, did he ever mention the name Margo to you?"

"No. Does it have anything to do with Fay's concern?"

"I don't think so, but I'm not sure. Thanks again for your help."

"No problem, Doc. She has done a terrific job and deserves the raise.

Within a few seconds there's a knock at the den door. In anticipation of who it is, Doc says, "Come on in, Mary."

Mary enters the room with a smile and asks, "Did you get your business done?"

Doc smiles, "Yes we're done. Now let's see those pictures."

Doc likes Bob and Mary and the pictures are really nice. He compliments them and they all leave the den together. Doc takes a round-about route to Bill.

Bill comments as Doc walks up. "Well, Doc, you really circulated. It took you almost an hour to get back. Everyone's having a great time. Did you find out who Margo is?"

"Not so loud."

Doc motions for Bill to follow him back to the den. Once inside, Doc says "Fay also noticed something was different, or should I say unusual, with Jack recently. He had a strange caller this week. It was a man, and Jack really got upset."

"Lot of help you are. I am still trying to figure out who this Margo is, and now a mysterious phone call from a man. We have some missing parts to the puzzle, if, in fact, we have a puzzle. I don't see any connection between the information we have."

Doc says, "I think I'll talk with Carol, maybe she knows this Margo."

"His ex-wife, is she here?"

"Yeah, she and her new husband came over. I asked Jack and he said it wouldn't bother him. Apparently, they have been friends the last few years and he has already met her new husband."

"Now that marriage was strange. As I recall, Jack and Carol were married less than two years."

"Eighteen months to be exact; I should remember; I was their best man. Remember when they broke up so soon there were rumors flying about implying Jack was gay?"

"Yeah, the press had a field day, vultures. While you were in with Bob and Mary, Pat said to tell you that a picture arrived from the lab. It came earlier, but, she forgot to tell you. Is it the one of Margo?"

"It should be. I had a copy made when they dried off the original to stabilize the water deterioration."

"Let me go with you, I may recognize her. And I want to see the Iceman's downfall."

"No, you stay here. I'll get the picture and come back."

Doc returns with the picture. He slides the copy out of the envelope. The print looks remarkable considering the condition of the original.

He hands the picture to Bill whose observations are obvious. "Well, I sure compliment him on his taste. She is beautiful and you were right, she is young, lucky bastard."

"Bill, you visit all our sites regularly to check on security. Do you recognize her? Maybe she is on our staff at one of our satellite offices?"

"No, Doc, believe me, I would remember her if I ever met her."

"Would you see if Carol is still here and ask her to see me, without her husband?"

"Sure."

In a few minutes, Carol comes into the den with Bill. Doc is studying the photo intently when they come in.

"Hi, Doc. Bill told me you wanted to see me."

Handing her the picture, Doc comments, "Carol, I need your help. I think Jack is in trouble."

Glancing at the photo, Carol responds with surprise, "With her? I don't believe it. She is beautiful, but he is too much of a gentleman to get mixed up with someone that young."

"I don't know, I thought you might shed some light on her identity. Perhaps someone you and Jack knew when you were married, one of his relatives? We only know her name is Margo, does that help?"

"No, I can't say I recognize her or the name."

Bill asks "Why did you two get divorced? He doesn't even date regularly yet."

Doc interjects before Carol feels she has to respond to Bill's comment. "Bill, I would appreciate it if you let me talk to Carol alone."

Bill realizes his comment was uncalled for. "Sure Doc. Sorry Carol, I didn't mean to pry. See you later."

After Bill leaves Carol speaks, "Before I answer, I want you to know, he was the most considerate person I have ever known. The problem was, I always felt like he was never satisfied; like I was being compared to someone. He never said anything, but he wouldn't have, to keep my feelings from being hurt. I just had this feeling, even though he was there all the time, he was not with me emotionally. It's hard to explain, yet you know it when happens. We parted as friends and he sincerely is happy that I remarried. He knew I was waiting to see if he would change and I finally gave up three years ago."

She hands the picture back to Doc. He is looking at the picture when he comments:

"If she could only speak."

"Let me see it again, Doc."

"Do you recognize her?"

"No, but she speaks volumes without saying a word."

"I must have missed something."

"Look at her clothes and hair style. A man might not notice, but she is either going to a masquerade party as someone from the late fifties or this picture was taken a long time ago."

Doc comes to realization, "If she was around twenty back in the late fifties, she would have been Jack's age at the time; but why such an old picture?"

"Maybe it's the only one he has. I bet her memory is what had him so preoccupied when we were married. She must have been real special to have a hold on him for all those years."

"That doesn't explain why the phone call that upset him was from a man."

"What phone call?"

"Nothing, really, thanks for letting me see the picture through a *woman's* eyes. I can't believe all the information you gave us from the clothes and hair style."

"Doc, please ask him if she, or his memory of her, is what came between us. We ladies like to know these things."

"I will, if the opportunity presents itself, but I think work was, and still is, his real mistress."

"Thanks Doc. I know you really tried to help us. Maybe we both just found out what the problem was. I'd take him back in a heartbeat if I wasn't married. He always did good by me. I found out he called my parents to make sure I was doing all right after we broke up."

"I know what you mean about him being a nice guy. I sure was disappointed that things didn't work out for the two of you; thanks again for your help."

"I still love him, Doc."

"What can I say, through the entire separation and even to today, he has never said anything negative about you. Frankly, Carol, I don't know if he can love anyone, but you were certainly good for him."

"Thanks. See you."

**Stromberger**

"Have a good weekend. I'll keep in touch."

After Carol leaves, Doc sticks his head out the door, gets Bill's attention and motions for him to come back in.

"Did you find out anything?"

"Bill, you aren't going to believe this. Carol pointed out several clues we missed on the picture. The girl is dressed for the late Fifties. Jack would have almost been that same age back then. I'll bet he knew her in that time frame and they were both the same age."

"Hell, you're no fun! I thought he was having a fling with a young chick."

"It still doesn't make sense that he wouldn't have a more recent picture. We still don't have a tie between the change in his character and the man on the phone last week causing him to get so irritated."

"Maybe it's some kind of blackmail scheme about her in his past. Not too many people know this, but I have written a program that can run checks on the individual corporate phone numbers."

"Bill, it would take days to go through and compare all his calls over the last six or eight weeks."

"Not really, Doc. I just finished a modification that allows me to identify all the outgoing and incoming numbers called during a given period that were not called previously. Fay told us this gut called last Thursday that should narrow it down to just a few. I will run it first thing Tuesday morning and let you know the results within one or two hours after I come in. Maybe this whole thing is a coincidence."

"Bill, there is one more piece to the puzzle I did not share with you earlier."

A note of betrayal crosses Bill's voice. "Why are you holding on me?"

"Frankly, I didn't want to let myself consider the option."

"Well, what is it.?"

"After he came up from emergency and was in his room unconscious, the attending doctor shared the results of his blood test. There were strong traces of an antihistamine, diphenhydramine, still in his blood; most likely from an overdose of sleeping pills."

"What, wouldn't that explain his being comatose after rescue?"

"It sure would. He probably would have died if he hadn't crashed when he did. The rescue and the heaving evacuated his stomach and neutralized the continued effect of the pills. The frogman said he tried to catch a bottle, thinking it was a prescription, but he lost it in the swirling water in the cabin as the plane went under. I'll bet they were sleeping pills."

Bill speculates, "Do you think he headed north on purpose so no one would find the plane?"

"I don't know Bill, but this sure is starting to look like it was planned and not an accident."

"It sure does, but it doesn't make sense. He has the world by the ass. There was no reason for him to do what we are now considering."

"I don't know, but let's face it, Friday morning we didn't know about Margo or the phone call. If he was trying to commit suicide and succeeded, we would have never looked. Don't forget, he did have her picture with him."

"I better go over to the office now and run that program."

"No need. He won't be out of the hospital until Tuesday at the earliest."

"You're right; I'll do it first thing when I get in Tuesday."

"Fine, now go out and have a good time at the party. We have given this enough time tonight."

Bill agrees, "Will do, Doc. Hey, I better get back to the lady from down your block. I think we were really hitting it off before this came up, and the night is still young."

"You really know how to pick them. She is a rich widow, but also is a prime suspect in her husband's early demise."

"Thanks, Doc. That really makes my night."

# EARLY SUNDAY MORNING AT DOC'S HOUSE

It's around 7:30 AM Sunday morning. The phone rings at Doc's house. Half awake, Doc glances at the clock. The early hour registers before he can grab the phone. During the couple seconds or so it takes to get the phone, a dozen reasons flash through his mind for someone to call such an early time; none of them are good! Considering the recent events he, is immediately convinced it is the hospital. He musters up a civil tone before picking up the phone and answers in a professional manner. "This is Doctor Bormes."

"Doc, this is Bill. I hate to wake you. I knew you would think it was the hospital, but this is important."

"It better be."

"I had a hard time sleeping last night so I came down to the office to run the phone audit we spoke about at your party last night. Jack had only ten first time contacts different from his call base in the last six weeks. I cross-checked with the incoming log and believe I found the one that upset him so much last Tuesday."

"Have you called it yet?"

"Yeah, and got an answering machine for a private detective named Peter Carpenter. I pulled some strings and got his unlisted home number. He has reluctantly agreed to meet at around nine this morning. Do you want to come?"

"Sure, thanks for calling. Come on over we will have breakfast here and then go and see him."

"Thanks, but I already had something. I will stop by and pick you up on the way there."

"Ok, but give me about an hour and I will be at the door."

"See you then."

Bill arrives right on schedule. Doc is waiting at the door with two travel cups of coffee. Getting in the, car he hands one to Bill. As soon as Doc is in the car he is all questions, "What did you ask him?"

"Not a thing, other than saying we wanted to see him regarding Jack's accident. I was surprised when he suggested this morning. I thought he would put us off until at least Tuesday. There must be some reason he suggested we meet early on Sunday morning – at his home."

"Hopefully he can shed some light on this Margo."

"Corporate sabotage and security is one thing, but to check on a friend, this is awkward."

"I know what you mean, considering what we suspect I feel we are doing the right thing. At least I think so."

"Maybe we should wait until after we see Jack, later this morning."

"Let's face it Bill, We both agree it looks like a suicide attempt. I think we should have as much background as possible before we meet with Jack."

They barely finish agreeing to continue with their task when they arrive at the detective's house. Carpenter comes to the door and escorts Bill and Doc into the family room. Before they can start the conversation Carpenter says, "Look gentlemen, I've been thinking since our phone call and I must take the stand that I cannot violate client privilege. I will not give you any details on the contract work I did for Mr. Burton. I agreed to see you because I thought Mr. Burton died. The morning news on TV said he survived. Why not ask him yourself?"

This is a totally different attitude than the friendly conciliatory person that agreed, almost rushed, to talk with them.

"Mr. Carpenter, I am Mr. Burton's doctor. We do expect to see Mr. Burton later today, but we had hoped your input could shed some light on some conflicting circumstances."

"I am sorry; doctor, but I can't divulge any details of my investigation without Mr. Burton's permission. I see no reason for our continuing this conversation. Good day."

Bill turns to Carpenter as they walk to the door. "Well, thanks for seeing us at such an early hour on a Sunday." Adding almost as an afterthought, "By the way, does a person named Margo figure in with this matter?"

"Gentlemen, I will not discuss any aspect of my investigation. You can ask him yourself when you see him."

There's a tone of sarcasm in Doc's parting comment. "It appears we drove all the way over here for nothing."

On the way to the hospital Bill comments. "Nice going Doc, we will be lucky if he ever talks to us again."

"Sorry, but he knew it was very important to us or we never would have come over on Sunday. I have to believe he knows something and suddenly he wouldn't budge."

"I guess I respect his position. After all we didn't explain our suicide theory, and we will be talking to Jack later today."

"We are close to the hospital. Why drive home and back? Let's stop at a restaurant and gather our thoughts over a cup of coffee, then go straight over to the hospital?"

"Sounds good to me."

The two spend at least an hour over a cup of coffee discussing all they have found out so far and trying to figure how the pieces fit to the puzzle, if there is one.

"Bill, we have to consider the possibility that the accident is not related to Margo. I'm thinking it would it be wise to deal with what we suspect to be a suicide attempt and deal with the Margo issue after he is released."

They leave the restaurant with mixed thoughts but agree that they must confront Jack; there may be a plausible explanation. They have decided it is more important to be honest and find out if their friend is in trouble. They hardly talk during the drive to the hospital.

# **DOC AND BILL GO TO THE TRAUMA CENTER**

In the elevator going up to Jack's floor, Bill asks, "Doc, how do we start?"

"I think we should let the conversation evolve naturally. He knows I am aware of Margo and he will get around to her sooner or later."

"What about our suspicions of a suicide attempt?"

"I think we should determine whether or not to bring it up, depending on how the conversation goes. What do you think?"

"Guess you're right, after all it is still a theory. I can't believe we're even considering it."

Exiting the elevator, Doc and Bill go straight to Mr. Burton's room.

"This is his room, twelve fifty-six."

Bill sticks his head in the door. "Hey, he isn't in."

"Probably down in therapy. He shouldn't be long. They have to give him lunch. Why don't you sit down while I check his chart?"

"Sure helps when you travel with a doctor. They can read those things."

"Wait a minute, this isn't his chart."

Bill responds, "Maybe they moved him."

Doc is worried. "You wait here; I'll go down to the nurses' station and check." They hadn't stopped on the way in because Doc knew Burton's room number from last night.

Several minutes' later Doc rushes back into the room. "I can't believe it. He apparently got dressed and just walked out sometime after they administered his pain medication around seven this morning. They realized he was missing around eight when they came in with his breakfast and found his hospital gown laying on the bed and his flight suit missing from the closet. They tried to call, but I forgot my damn cell phone at home."

"I thought you said he wouldn't be checked out until Tuesday."

"That's what they told me, but apparently he just walked out!"

"I'll call his apartment."

"You can call on the way over. We better find out why he left. Now I am worried."

**Stromberger**

"Right, Doc."

## **DOC AND BILL RACE TO BURTON'S CONDO**

Bill's driving scares the hell out of Doc. If a light isn't green, he runs it. They arrive at the Jack's posh condo in record time.

Leaving the car in the visitors parking area, Doc and Bill walk with a quick pace to the main entrance. As they enter the lobby, the desk manager, Dennis, does not recognize them and asks, "Good morning, gentlemen, how may I help you?"

Doc responds, "I am Dr. Bormes, Mr. Burton's personal physician. We are here to see him about his medication."

"I will have to ring to see if he is expecting you."

They wait for what seems an eternity while the desk manager tries in vain to get an answer from Jack's apartment.

"Gentlemen, Mr. Burton does not answer, he must be out. Would you care to leave a message?"

Doc replies, "He could also have passed out from the medication. It is imperative we see if he is all right. I trust you are aware of his plane accident."

"I certainly am, I am only following our procedures, let me call the manager for you."

"Thanks, I apologize for being short but he has gone through a lot the last few days."

"I understand, we were worried when we heard the news; here comes Mr. Peterson now." He introduces Doc. "Mr. Peterson, this is Dr. Bormes, Mr. Burton's doctor. There is a question of his medication and they would like you to take them up to make sure everything's all right. Correct, gentlemen?"

Doc responds, "Yes, and thank you for your help."

After checking Doc and Bill's identification, Mr. Peterson is uncomfortable with the circumstance but lets them through the security gate. He mumbles all the way up on the elevator, but directs them to Jack's door. Doc tries the bell several times with no response.

The manager comments, "He's obviously not answering, perhaps he went out for a walk."

"As sore as he is, I doubt if he's out walking. You have heard of his plane crash. My concern is that he cannot answer the bell." Doc continues in a tone that won't accept no for an answer, "For all we know he may be unconscious and I need you to open this door, now."

"This is highly irregular, but you are his doctor."

# **UNITED FLIGHT 659 TO SEATTLE**
## (Just about an hour out of Chicago)

The cabin attendant is making an announcement to the passengers for a second time since they departed from Chicago.

"Ladies and gentlemen, as you can tell we have finally passed the turbulence. The Captain has informed me that we will have the cloud cover below almost all the way to Seattle. You can loosen you seat belts and move around the cabin if you choose, but please keep your belt on when you are seated. We may encounter more turbulence without notice."

Burton is seated in first class and has been asleep since a few minutes after take-off. He is still exhausted from the ordeal just two days ago. He slept through the first announcement but for some reason this one has awakened him. He gets up to go to the bathroom and realizes just how sore he is.

After walking less than 20 feet, he is recognized by several of the passengers who have seen his picture on most of the business magazine covers. He returns to his seat immediately after using the bathroom. He would have preferred to stretch his sore legs more, but he has already been stopped twice by people who want to engage in idle conversation about his crash and upcoming promotion.

He slides his club bag out from under the seat and removes a new portable Walkman cassette player that he bought at the airport to replace the older Webcor that he lost in the crash. He also takes out four cassettes he picked up at his apartment. They all have hand written end labels like the ones he lost in the crash. These are tapes he prerecorded from individual sound tracks that had strong meaning to him at some point in his life. A smile crosses his face as he reads the labels; The Lettermen, Johnnie Mathis, Everly Brothers, Elvis, Connie Francis, Four Preps, Beach Boys. The songs were popular in the late Fifties, through the mid Sixties, when he was in the Army. He selects one, places it into the player and pushes the play button. As the music begins, he stares out the window trying to get lost in the cloud formations.

## **DOC AND BILL GAIN ACCESS TO BURTON'S CONDO**

Reluctantly opening the door, the manager stands at the threshold calling, "Mr. Burton, Mr. Burton, are you all right?"

Instinctively, Doc and Bill walk him and into the condo.

"Bill, you check out the kitchen and the forward rooms. I'll go to the bedrooms and back baths. Hope to hell he isn't just taking a shower."

The manager calls out as they walk by. "I don't know if this is proper."

Bill turns and addresses the manager's comment. "We will take responsibility if anything goes wrong. What if he is laying in the back unconscious?"

"Well, I guess it's all right, but just to check on him."

After a quick look, Bill calls to Doc in the back of the condo. "Doc, he's not in the kitchen or living room."

Doc calls from the rear of the condo, "He's not in any of the bedrooms either."

"Then where the hell is he?" As Bill continues to look in the front area, "Maybe he didn't come here after all."

Doc calls from the master bedroom. "Bill, come here."

As Bill enters, Doc comments, "He's been here." pointing at the hospital bag on the floor with his flight suit. "But it looks like he didn't even lie down in the bed."

Walking into the master bath, Bill calls out, "Looks like he showered, there's wet towels in the bathroom."

Doc notices something on the kitchen table, "Here's an envelope with a note on the table addressed to someone named Martha."

"Come on, Doc, first Margo and now Martha."

The manager, still standing at the threshold, speaks up, "Perhaps I can help with Martha; she's his cleaning lady. She works for several residents in the building."

"Why would he leave her an envelope?"

The Manager responds, "Probably instructions on how he wants something done."

Walking into the kitchen Bill suggests, "Doc you better open it and find out what's inside."

"Bill, look at this note. He is thanking her for all the years of service and has left a check for $25,000 for her son's college. Why would you leave it in an envelope and not give it to her in person?"

"You would, Doc, if you were in a hurry and never intended to see her again! Hey, wait a minute. If our suicide theory is correct, that explains his comments to Fay and the urgency to get her raise finalized before he took off Friday."

The Manager comments, "Are you suggesting Mr. Burton tried to commit suicide?"

Doc ignores the manager's comments. "It all fits, except we don't know about this Margo."

"Get Langman on the phone and bring him up to date. He usually stays at the Indy Suites. I will look around some more to see if we missed something."

The manager is still standing just inside the condo doorway protesting when Bill takes him by the arm and escorts him out into the hall, "Thanks for your help, Mr. Peterson," as he closes the door, leaving the manager standing in the hall protesting.

Bill then resumes his search for clues as to where Jack has gone. Doc gets Mr. Langman on the phone unexpectedly fast. He is just finishing bringing him up to date on what they have found when Bill calls to him from the den.

"Doc, I found a card with a travel agent's number out on the desk. I will call them on the second line."

Minutes later, Bill rushes into the room while Doc is on the phone with Mr. Langman. Bill interrupts; "Doc they said he left for Seattle over an hour ago and the next flight isn't for three hours."

Doc asks. "Did you hear that, sir?"

Doc listens to Mr. Langmans response then replies; "All right, we'll get started as soon as I hang up, and keep you updated as we go."

"Go where?" As if Bill hasn't already guessed.

Doc hangs up the phone, "We're going to Seattle. He said his Grumman should be back by now. He wants us to start for Seattle as soon as we can."

Bill asks, "Where in Seattle?"

"I don't know. He will have our people working on this end to get more information, but we have to start as soon as possible. It's a three-or four-hour trip and Jack already has over an hour head start. They will update us in transit. You call the hangar at O'Hare and see if Mr. Langman's Grumman is back from Indianapolis."

"Well at least we are going in style." Bill calls the company crew room at O'Hare. "Hello, let me talk to Rick Lee." After a short conversation he finds Doc in the living room. "Boy, we sure got the royal treatment. Langman already called and released his plane to us for the trip. I talked to Rick, he said they were refueling the Grumman and he should be at Meigs within an hour."

"My only plans for the weekend was the party last night. How about you, Bill?"

"I don't have any, but you better call home. Pat may have something planned you don't know about."

"Meigs is less than 15 minutes away, so we've got some time before we have to leave to catch the Grumman. You start checking out the place to see if there is any indication where Jack is headed in Seattle. I'll join you after I call Pat."

## **BACK ONBOARD FLIGHT 659**

Mr. Burton spends a few minutes staring out the window at the blanket of clouds below. Then, glancing back at the tape player, he presses the PLAY button.

The first song was "Where or When" by the Lettermen. A warm smile comes over his face as the music starts. The words seem to ease the lingering discomfort in his legs from the brief walk to the bathroom. He slips back in time to his first Christmas at home in Chicago after getting out of the Army in 1959.

*He recalls driving down Cicero Avenue headed to Midway Airport. It was just after 5:00 AM. The 30-mile trip from his home in Mt. Greenwood went faster than he could ever remember. After all, it was the Saturday of a Christmas weekend, with Christmas falling on Monday. Everyone who had to travel had already departed by Friday and the local visits would not start until Sunday or Monday. The weather was typical for a Christmas in Chicago: 29 degrees, with wind gusts to 35 mph. They had a light three inches of powdery snow last night, and the cold kept it crystalline that sparkled like diamonds in his headlights. It would stay for a few days and the kids would delight in trying out their new sleds and skates after Christmas.*

*It was the beginning of a beautiful day; the cold made the air crystal clear and gave him an unobstructed view of the aircraft on their final approach. In the east, the sun started expanding a thin ribbon of light gold along the powder-blue horizon.*

*Margo would arrive on the 6:30 AM flight from Seattle. The plan was for her to stay for a week to get a chance to meet his parents and share the holiday. Last year he was in the Army and had spent Christmas at her house in Pacific Shores, Washington. He never dreamed then that they would be together this Christmas at his house in Chicago.*

*It was 5:30 when he turned into the near-empty Midway Airport parking lot. He parked within one hundred feet of the United Airline entrance with almost an hour to spare. He opened the car door only to be immediately reminded of how the heater had spared him from the weather outside. He decided to leave the doors unlocked to make sure they could get in quickly when they returned. He jumped out and was half-way to the United doors when he realized hed had forgotten his mother's car-coat in the back seat. She had sent it just in case Margo didn't anticipate the extreme difference between the Seattle and Chicago weather. He paused and then returned to the car to get the coat. He had left his gloves at home and his hand burned from the cold steel door handle. Grabbing the coat, he hastily headed again toward the doors to the lobby with their promise of warmth and protection from the weather. Finally he reached the doors; in one motion he opened them and thrust himself into the lobby, standing for a minute rubbing his hands in an attempt to stimulate the circulation and hasten the penetration of the heat. There were a few employees behind the ticket counters and just a handful of travelers. At the United desk he confirmed her 6:30 flight was on time.*

*He walked over to a small coffee shop situated next to her arrival gate. His hands were only now warming up as he entered the coffee shop.*

*The lone waitress was slender, with long blonde hair, in her mid-20's at most, who was glad to have some company. He ordered a hot chocolate, which seemed more comforting than coffee on a morning this cold. The waitress started the conversation when she served him, asking, "What brought you out on a morning like this?"*

*She was very patient as he took over the conversation. He told her he was meeting Margo and then spent several minutes telling her how great she was. The waitress said, "She must think you are special to come here over Christmas." They continued to talk about the weather and their individual holiday plans.*

*The coffee shop had a large picture window with a commanding view of the field and the gate area where Margo's flight would be arriving. He realized her flight was close when he noticed the activity around the tarmac just in front of her gate area. The baggage carts were pulled by a little tractor with a driver bundled up like a snow man. There was very little defense on the flat, open tarmac from the 'Hawk', a name given the winter wind in Chicago when it drives the cold like an icicle right through your body. The rolling stairway was being positioned for the plane's arrival. Checking his watch, he realized it was about twenty minutes before her arrival.*

## **BACK AT MR. BURTON'S CONDO**

Doc finished the call to Pat and joined Bill in the search for some indication as to where Jack is headed in Seattle. He is in the living room going through some correspondence on a small table when Bill calls to him.

"Doc, come into the den."

"What's up, did you find something?"

"It's more what I didn't find. Look at his gun collection on the wall. This empty space, if I remember correctly, is for his Glock Pistol."

"We are right; he is trying to kill himself."

"Not really, Doc. He could have pulled the trigger right here in the privacy of his own den."

"Are you thinking what I am? He could be going to kill this Margo. Hey, wait a minute. When Carol looked at Margo's picture she commented on the background scenery. I thought it was possibly Wisconsin or Michigan, but it sure could have been the Pacific Northwest"

"That might explain the trip to Seattle." Pointing to the cassette rack, he continues. Oh, as I was nosing around I noticed some tapes missing from the rack. I came over a few months ago to help him set up a system to convert his old tapes to CD's. According to the index they are several missing; 'Oldies and Goodies', 'Dearest Burgie' and a couple others that he seems to have taken with him."

"Did you say a tape titled 'Dearest Burgie'?"

"That's what it says. He told me he liked re-recording hard-to-find tracks that he enjoyed. The music and artists were mixed on a tape and he wanted to convert them to CD's. I helped him set up a basic index protocol for the CD's."

"Perhaps the index is on his laptop. I'll bet it's password protected."

"I am sure it is, but there are several sheets of printed index excerpts here on the shelf."

"I bet the 'Dearest Burgie' track is the one we want."

Bill is scrolling down the index sheets. "Here it is, 'Dearest Burgie', its track 18 on CD number 36." Bill is going through the CD file when he hits pay dirt. "Here it is: CD number 36. I'm not sure we want to know what is on this CD, know

## Stromberger

what I mean? This must be extremely personal, and in a way I feel we are stepping beyond our friendship."

"I think we better listen to it. It may give us some indication of what's going on or at least a clue as to who she is."

Bill reluctantly agrees, "I guess it's all right."

Bill still appears uncomfortable as he turns on the CD player and places the CD on the slide out player tray. As the CD disappears into the player they both seem uneasy feeling, perhaps their friend has a dark side.

After a moment's hesitation, Bill punches track 18 into the keyboard selector. Neither man glances at the other. They are both transfixed on the CD player.

Suddenly the velvet voice of a young lady who sounds a bit confused at first pours out of the speakers.

*"Dearest Burgie, I don't know how to start. I can't afford to come and see you and I don't want to hear the hurt*

in your voice, so I won't call. I feel terrible about telling you this way, but I can at least get all of it out without interruptions. Please try to forgive me for what I am about to tell you.

I met a person on the plane coming back to Seattle after visiting your family last Christmas. We have been seeing each other for three months and then last week..."

Her voice shows hesitation and anxiety, mixed with remorse for what she was about to say. She continues.

"...I don't know how to say this. I know we promised to finish school, and we made plans for our future. This is one of these things that just happens. Please believe me; I never set out to hurt you. I can't explain what happened. Maybe I just don't want to wait for two more years. This may sound crazy, especially now, but I will always cherish the memories of our times together. You are *a wonderful person and I cannot tell you how much I regret this situation.*

*Please don't call; it will only be harder on both of us to accept the circumstances. I am already married and will have moved out of state by the time you get this tape. I told my family that I don't want you to know where I am. You have to believe this is the hardest thing I have ever done. You deserve someone better, and I know that God will take care of you. I only hope He can forgive me for what I have done."*

"Christ, Bill! She sent him a 'Dear John' on a cassette tape. I think we just found out why he took the gun."

"I can't figure out when she sent the tape. Was it back then or recently?"

"She references visiting his family at Christmas and going to college. It must have been just after he got out of the Army."

"Look at the time. We better leave for Meigs. The Grumman is due pretty soon."

"Yeah, I forgot the time with everything going on, and now this."

## **LUNCH ONBOARD FLIGHT 659**

The cabin attendant first thought she recognized him from his pictures on the business magazine covers, then referenced the passenger manifest to confirm that he is Mr. Burton. Realizing he is daydreaming she asks quietly, "Excuse me, you seem lost in your music, but would you be interested in lunch, Mr. Burton?" Adding in a seductive tone, "Or should I call you 'Iceman', pointing to a business magazine with his picture on the cover that she is carrying back to the rack. "You sure look good, considering your incident just a few days ago."

"I am a little sore yet, but I am living proof that only the good die young."

"Please let me know if there is anything we can get for your discomfort."

"Thanks, I'll keep that in mind."

"Would you care for lunch now? I didn't want to bother you earlier. "

"Thanks, but I really don't feel hungry right now."

"Perhaps later."

"I would appreciate that."

He is seated next to a window. As she leaves, he looks out again at the heavy clouds that deny him even a glimpse of the passing countryside below. How ironic, he put millions of miles on board the corporate jets and can't remember simply looking out the window to enjoy the view.

He realizes just how much of life he truly never took time to enjoy, like this simple act of enjoying the view from a plane. It doesn't take long, and he has drifted back to listening to the music. Turning toward the window again, he stares at the cloud cover to minimize distractions from within the plane. The next song on the tape is "The Twelfth of Never" by Johnny Mathis. It was among the songs they played when he brought Margo back to Midway for her return flight after her Christmas visit.

They were standing in the gate area but close enough to the hall to hear the jukebox play their selections.

*They only had seven days, but plans were made for their entire future.*

*He had his arms around her shoulders. She seemed to fit under his arms like a piece in a puzzle. Without saying a word, they spoke volumes with their eyes. Christmas had gone extremely well. His parents could not have been more pleased. Their departure from his house an hour ago was filled with hugs, kisses and a few tears from his mother.*

*His parents had no idea of the plans he and Margo made that Christmas. They didn't tell anyone, but they had decided to get married as soon as they finished school, in just under two years. He was already assured of a job with OMNI, a large, multi-faceted corporation. He was working part time while attending school and they really liked him. Their plans also included him making a trip to Seattle during the upcoming summer. She would start sending applications to local Chicago hospitals half-way through her final year* and come back to do interviews during her next visit.

There was a relaxed feeling. They hated to part, but realized that their future together would be started as soon as they finished the challenges of school that lay ahead.

They were consciously aware that the plane was loading, but neither wanted to acknowledge the pending separation. She snuggled in the comfort of his encircled arms, saying softly:

"This moment, and the last week, will help me endure the months without you."

"I feel the same way, dear," he replied while pulling a cassette from his jacket pocket. "I recorded this tape with some personal messages for you to hear while we are apart." Adding with a gleam in his eye, "Be sure you are alone when you play it."

"Now I know why you gave me that tape recorder. It wasn't just to *record lectures, but to punish me with an endless number of cold showers I have to take after listening to one of those tapes." Adding with a smile, "But, don't stop sending them."*

*Burgie said with a gleam in his eye, "When are you going to send me one?"*

*"I know. I just haven't worked up the courage to put my inner feelings on tape. We will have the rest of our lives together. I know it seems unfair to have to wait to start."*

*"I know. Hey, I noticed there's a flight departing for Las Vegas just down the hall. What do you say we catch it and get married today?"*

*"That isn't fair. You know I would, but let's keep our priorities straight. I guess I will be the one who has to keep things in perspective."*

*"Yeah, I guess I am a little impulsive."*

*She replied with a devilish smile, "Boy, are you in for a surprise. I have been taking notes and will collect all these promises once we are married."*

*With a devilish grin, Burgie said, "I will remind you of that comment on our honeymoon."*

*She snuggled closer and in a seductive voice responded. "You won't have to remind me."*

*"If you want to be a little more explicit, we could still catch the plane for Vegas."*

*"You are unbelievable." Margo drew her grip on his waist, pulling them closer, "God, we are going to have a wonderful life together."*

*The gate agent had been patient, sensing these last moments were very special to the young couple. Finally she made an announcement for all passengers to board. Margo was the only passenger left in the gate area. The* others have been on board for a few minutes.

They gave each other a strong and long squeeze. Relaxing her grip, she whispered: "Burgie, I have to leave."

"I know, and I am not making it any easier." He relaxed his arms and they slowly started toward the doors to the tarmac and the waiting plane. She turned to him at the bottom of the steps, "You know I love you, and I always will. Remember what I wrote on the picture. 'Wherever we are, we will always be together'." She gave him one last kiss and turned quickly to head up the stairs.

Turning for a moment as she reached the top, she waved and then went quickly inside the door and out of sight.

The ground crew locked the door and moved the stairs away from the plane. The small tractor started to push the plane away from the gate. He searched the windows to catch a glimpse *of her. He cannot identify her, but waved in case she could see him.*

*All too soon, the large four-engine prop plane slowly lumbered down the taxiway out of sight. He caught a fast glimpse as it passed across the field on take-off.*

The memory of that day and the entire week of commitments and promises for a shared future brings a wave of mixed emotions. First sensual, at the memory of her petite body snuggled tightly inside his circled arms. Her devilish smile, with a look of love that promised passion. Then sadness, at the lost paradise he felt was secured during that brief Christmas week. Finally, hostility, grief and betrayal at the way so many years were twisted and wasted.

He forces himself to withdraw from his thoughts and focuses on the clouds that cover the entire area below the plane. He drifts off to sleep for almost an hour until he is awakened by the cabin attendant. She has his food tray.

"We're not that far from Seattle, I thought you might like something now while you still have time to enjoy your meal."

"Thanks for remembering. I would enjoy something now."

He has a hard time finishing the meal. Occasionally, he stares out the window to lose his thoughts in the different cloud formations.

## **BILL AND DOC ARRIVE AT MEIGS FIELD**

Doc and Bill arrive at Meigs Field. Doc's wife, Pat, is already there. She is waiting at the small terminal building reception area.

Doc calls out as they walk up, "Hi, dear, I sure am glad you could make it. Have you got the clothes?"

"I certainly hope you don't mind my selection. Hi, Bill. I understand you two are headed for Seattle. Make sure he doesn't get in trouble."

"Will do, Pat."

"What has happened to Jack? Have you guys got any ideas where he is?"

Doc replies, "Supposedly, we will get his final destination information on the way there."

Bill adds, "It's going to be a difficult search if we don't."

Pat questions again, "Who's this Margo? Do you really think he is going to kill her too? God, I can't believe I said that."

Bill says, "We both started out skeptical about many aspects of that theory, but it sure looks

## Stromberger

like a possibility after hearing a copy of a tape she sent him."

Doc adds, "If we don't find her before he does, they could both be dead. It just doesn't seem real, but Bill pointed out he doesn't have to go to Seattle if he only intends to kill himself, and this tape really cinched it."

Pat inquires, "Tell me about the tape."

Doc answers, "We don't have time now, but I will go over it later."

"Bill, what are you going to do for a change of clothes?"

He replies, pointing to a travel bag he is carrying, "I fit in Jack's, so I raided his closet. Probably the most expensive clothes I will ever wear."

"Bill, it just dawned on me. Jack took off from here two days ago and no one guessed he had a care in the world."

"Doc, you better tell Pat about the tape while I go over to the tower and see if they heard from our plane."

Bill is gone only a short time and comes back with some haste in his step.

"How far out are they?"

"They said very soon. In fact it looks like them over there on their final approach over Shedd Aquarium now. Let me take your bag, Doc. I'll let you two say your good byes. Meet you out on the taxi area, don't be too long. They will want us on board as soon as possible. Goodbye, Pat, see you later."

Bill takes their bags out to the taxi area. He isn't there long when the sleek Grumman corporate jet touches down on the short runway. From the noise of the reverse thrusters on the engines, Bill can tell they really did not have much room to spare. The Grumman turns at the very end of the runway and makes another turn to come along the taxi-way toward the transit parking area where Bill is waiting.

Bill turns to look for Doc just as he joins him. Without hesitation, the pilot taxies over to the waiting men. The co-pilot lowers the stairs and calls for them to come on board. They scurry up the steps and are quickly strapped in because they are cleared to return to the active runway and take off as soon as they are ready.

The co-pilot finalizes securing the door and calls forward to the cockpit; "They're strapped in, let's roll."

On his way to the cockpit, the copilot apologizes, "Sorry for the rush, but we will be back to see you as soon as we are airborne and out of the traffic pattern."

The pilot, Rick Lee, looking through the open cockpit door, yells back. "Hi, Doc, Bill; I can't wait to get the low down but we have to get out of here now. Be busy for fifteen minutes and then I'll be back. Hang on, we have to really power up to get off this short runway."

By now they have taxied back to the active runway and the copilot has returned to the cockpit. Within seconds the Grumman accelerates down the runway. When they finally lift off, they climb at a steep angle straight away from the city and then swing west toward Seattle. As promised, it's about 15 minutes before they are in level flight and Rick comes back to talk with Doc and Bill.

"Hi guys, like the take-off?"

"I know you were a carrier pilot, but you really didn't have to prove it. For a while there, I thought Doc was going to lose it."

"The old man really made it sound important, so I did a quick turn-around at Meigs so we could avoid the paper-work delays. He said to get you two to Seattle in a hurry. What's the emergency?"

"Doc, you better bring him up to date. I will call corporate and see if they have a clue where Jack is headed in Seattle."

"Jack Burton? I thought he was in the hospital recovering from his plane crash."

Doc starts to give him some background while Bill calls the office for an update. Bill returns as Doc is finishing.

"Well, they're going to fetch that PI, Carpenter, and see if they can convince him that he better forget client privilege considering the recent turn of events. Hope they have some answers before we start wandering the streets of Seattle without a clue as to where to look."

Rick questions inquisitively, "You mean you have no idea where he is going in Seattle?"

"That's right, and you are racing to get us there as close as possible to his arrival time. The only thing we know for sure is that he has almost a two-hour head start."

"Well, we can shave off almost an hour, not much more."

Doc jokes. "Hell, all he has to do is be out of sight, if you don't know where to look. Like Bill pointed out at Meigs, Seattle is a big town."

"I better get back up front. You might as well settle in, it will take us at least two and a half hours. Check the galley; I had the commissary throw in some provisions while we flight checked the plane. I can't guarantee anything. We didn't have much time before we left."

Doc responds, "That's fine; we really aren't that hungry."

"Speak for yourself, Doc; I am going to see what's back there. Do you guys want coffee up front?"

Walking toward the cockpit, Rick responds with a smile. "That would be great. I like passengers who take care of the crew."

## ONBOARD THE GRUMMAN TWO HOURS OUT OF O'HARE

They are above the clouds and the trip has been smooth so far. Rick is back in the galley talking with Doc and Bill about their upcoming search for Burton in Seattle.

Bill is just saying, "Can you believe this, Rick? We aren't that far from Seattle and haven't heard yet if they are making any progress with the private investigator."

"You and Doc may be coming home with us if they can't get him to tell where Jack is headed."

Just then the copilot, Tom Peters, calls back from the cockpit, "Captain I was just informed by SeaTac" (Seattle/Tacoma Airport) "that they are experiencing extreme delays because of heavy fog."

"Thanks, Tom, I'll be right up."

Doc speculates. "That's great; it may delay his landing so we can make up some time."

"Not necessarily Doc" says Rick. "We are usually all delayed the same amount of time. Our biggest problem is if they have slipped into SeaTac ahead of the really bad stuff and we get blocked. I'll check on the situation and keep you updated."

The phone rings, "There's the phone Doc, I'll get it. Hello, this is Bill. Hope you have some good news for a change" --- "You've got to be kidding! Then play hardball with him. Tell Carpenter he can be charged as an accessory to murder because we have more than enough evidence that Jack is also going to kill her." --- "That's right, accessory to murder. Call us back, and it better be soon, we're not that far from Seattle."

Hanging up the phone in disgust, Bill comments to Doc, "God, I wish I was there. Do you believe it, Doc? This PI is still holding his ground. They took him up to the executive dining room to try and schmooze him with a meal!"

"Bill, we better get something soon. They said we're about an hour from SeaTac."

"At least that's good news. We made up some real time on him."

Rick calls from the cockpit, "Doc, Bill, you better come up here."

Bill asks as they enter the cockpit, "What's the news about the weather, Rick?"

"Well, there's bad news and worse news. Which one do you want first?"

Doc answers, "Give us the bad news first."

"The fog is so bad that SeaTac has closed the field. Jack's flight was one of the last commercial flights to get clearance to land."

Bill questions, "What could be worse?"

Rick responds with frustration in his voice. "Until further notice, the field is open to commercial traffic only – we're private. I tried to bully my way in with the corporate jet routine but no dice, sorry. You must have a fuel emergency, and we don't. SeaTac recommends we divert to Portland or Spokane."

# BURTON REACHES SEATTLE AND CATCHES THE FERRY

Jack had taken some pain meds about an hour before arriving in Seattle. As he gets up to exit the aircraft, it is apparent that they haven't taken full effect. For the first few minutes he has a stiff and gated stride until the full mobility is restored. He retrieves his small roller bag from the carousel and continues to the Avis Car rental area. He stops to pick up a map and verifies the location of his vehicle.

His legs welcome the needed exercise as he traverses the parking area. The discomfort is much less pronounced, the pain meds are finally taking effect. The fresh air feels great, even though it is heavy with fog. A glimmer of peace comes to his face as the cool moist air fills his lungs. The stiffness in his legs is disappearing as he walks to the car.

He's in no rush and wants to stand a little before sitting again so he opens the map on the trunk of the car and takes his time reviewing the route highlighted by the Avis agent. The route takes him south around the bottom of Everett Bay, through Tacoma and Olympia, then directly west on the long drive to Hoquiam and the Pacific Ocean. A turn north on coast highway 109 takes him past several small towns and finally to his destination, Pacific Shores.

Taking a few minutes more to review the map, he thinks to himself, *Why am I worried about time, I have my whole life to get there. Why not retrace the route Margo and I took to her house that Christmas Eve when I was in the Army?*

Running his finger along the map, he traces the revised route, the one he and Margo took. He will head toward Seattle on I5. Then down to the docks and across Elliott Bay by Ferry to Bremerton. From Bremerton he traces the drive as it winds the back roads west toward the ocean until he breaks out onto the main road to Hoquiam and Aberdeen. It will take a little longer, but what's the rush? Before starting, he removes several cassettes from his flight bag and places them on the passenger's seat.

Exiting SeaTac Airport he finds the I5 North ramp. The first sign, barely visible in the fog, reads, "Seattle 20 miles". Though a short distance, the fog will command a somewhat longer driving time. Years of commercial development have dramatically changed the view along his route but the fog obscures all but a few structures along the highway. The limited visibility requires all his attention while driving and he is happy to finally see the sign marked "Ferry Docks and Kingdome Exit." The exit ramp drops sharply from the elevated expressway to the dock area. None of this was in place when they took the trip years ago. Everything is new and, at first, a little confusing. The fog doesn't help either. Finally, the ramp comes to the harbor level, and he sees an arrow directing him to Ferry Docks.

It only takes a few minutes before he arrives at the dock and drives to the toll booth.

The attendant asks, "What is your destination?"

"Bremerton, please."

"Round trip, or one way?"

The reality of what he is contemplating, strikes him. After a moment, he finally responds, "One way, please."

"That will be $7.50, please; your ferry leaves in 15 minutes. Please pull up behind the last car in aisle 12."

"Aisle 12, right?"

He cautiously negotiates his way to aisle 12. The fog prohibits his view of the ferry, even though it is enormous, holding 200 cars, and is docked only 150 or so feet away. After a short wait the parking attendant suddenly seems to appear magically from the fog and directs the line of waiting cars toward the loading ramp. He is concentrating on the vehicles in front and watching the ramp to the ferry before realizing he is on board and being positioned for parking. Once parked, he exits the car and heads up the stairs to the upper decks.

Stopping, almost instinctively, at cafeteria on the enclosed mid-deck, to pick up a cup of hot chocolate. Most of the passengers opt for the comfort of and protection from the weather and take seats on the mid-deck. He continues up to the top deck, over 50 feet above the barely visible water below. The fog is so thick that the front of the 250-foot ferry, and the beautiful Seattle skyline that towers above the dock area, is barely visible. The most he can make out are ghostly shadows of the taller buildings; perhaps it's better not to see the changes. It would only remind him how much he has missed in life. He notices a young couple along the railing, maybe 100 feet away. They are defined only by the color of their clothes, made soft by the fog, hardly more than just two silhouettes. It reminds him of their trip, standing there with his hot chocolate, that day starts to come back to him.

## **DOC AND BILL FINALLY HAVE A DESTINATION**

Bill asks, "Does that mean we have to go to either Spokane or Portland, or can we land somewhere else?"

Rick replies, "We can land anywhere we can reach on our fuel plus a reserve and a long enough runway."

Doc asks, "How far can we safely go?"

"I have enough fuel to reach the Pacific Coast and then some."

"I suggest we look for a closer alternate; perhaps west of Seattle?" says Doc.

"You know, you have a point. Our only problem is this baby needs quite a bit of asphalt to stop. That eliminates most small fields, but Tom and I will start checking the maps."

Just then the phone rings. Bill leaves the cockpit to answer it. "This is Bill." Doc notices Bill's expression change almost immediately to a smile. The voice at the other end must have brought a ray of sunlight to an otherwise emotionally gloomy day.

With a positive voice Bill says, "I'm glad; Carpenter has finally given in a little. Just what did he tell us?" --- "You must be kidding. That's all? What about this Margo?" --- "What do you mean, nothing?"

Bill's voice is starting to show his frustration again. "But he did tell you Jack is probably headed for a small town on the Pacific Coast, wait, let me write this down. 'Pacific Shores', directly west of Seattle and north along the coast. Got it, at least we have some idea where he is going. We have to find an alternate airport because of the fog." --- "No, unfortunately, we only know he has landed in Seattle already. Is there anything else?" --- "OK, keep us posted, we should be in the plane for at least another hour or so."

Bill heads for the cockpit with his scribbled note. "Find Pacific Shores on the map."

Everyone is in the cockpit, which has room for two or three but all four are trying to search the map at one time.

Tom finds it. "Here it is, Pacific Shores," he points it out. "It's along the coast almost straight west of Seattle and then 20 or so miles north. Now all we need is an airport along the coast."

"If we land along the coast we can pick up some time," observes Doc, "Jack has to drive west from Seattle."

Rick says, "You're right, but remember, we need a decent length runway for this bird."

Tom interrupts, "Wait, I found one. Let me see how their weather is. We'll need better conditions because most small fields don't have Ground Control Approach equipment."

It is obviously too crowded in the cockpit, so Doc and Bill move back into the cabin. Rick and Tom do not need any distractions while they search the map for air fields with runways long enough to accommodate the Grumman.

After they sit down, Doc says, "How ironic."

"What do you mean?"

"The plane that allowed us to make up time is now a barrier to our getting down."

About fifteen minutes later, Rick calls back from the cockpit, "Good news, we found one, Shepard Field. It's on the coast and south of Pacific

Shores. They said the fog hasn't burned off yet and they have some wet spots on the runway which will make out landing tricky.

They also confirmed the coastline is clear all the way to Pacific Shores. I set you up with a helicopter from Shepard Field to Ocean Shores which should be there by the time we land. Overall, we should pick up some time on Jack."

## BURTON ON THE UPPER DECK OF THE FERRY DEPARTING FROM SEATTLE

Jack still has a clear memory of that day.

*He had picked her up at St. Joseph's School of Nursing in Tacoma around 8:15 AM on Christmas Eve. She stayed an extra day after the rest of the class had left for Christmas break in order to accompany him on the ride to her house. After briefly exchanging holiday greetings with the limited staff on duty at St. Joseph's, they departed for the holiday at her house. She lived in Pacific Shores and wanted to give him some company on the long ride, plus she certainly liked being with him.*

*They decided there was plenty of time, so they drove to Seattle. It was just a few miles out of their way, and would be well worth the extra time to enjoy the ferry trip from Seattle to Bremerton. It was a perfect winter day; the sun was out and the temperature was almost 60, with crispness in the air. Traffic was light going to Seattle and the ride took no time at all, nothing like his drive today. They were in luck, and drove onto the ferry almost as soon as they arrived, much like he did today. That was his first experience driving aboard a ferry, and the sensation was more like driving into the mouth of a large fish. He was directed into position by a deckhand. Once parked, they were allowed to leave the car and go to the upper decks.*

*They climbed the stairs, stopping only at the mid deck just long enough to buy hot chocolates. Continuing up the stairs, they came out on the top deck. At first, the Seattle skyline towered over the ferry. They were just casting off, and the warm sunlight was interrupted only by the cool shadows made by the taller buildings, sweeping across the deck as the ferry moved through their path on* departure. The city slowly became more manageable in a single view as they moved farther from shore, almost as if they were looking through a zoom lens. Soon, the entire skyline was just like the picture on the post cards being sold in the lounge area below. They were almost alone on the top deck in the fresh air. All but a few people were down in the enclosed deck below, but they weren't in love and finding warmth in the mere presence of their companionship. They stood close together at the railing, watching the city become smaller by the moment, a cup of hot chocolate in one hand and the other arm firmly around the other's waist. They stood there for 20 minutes not saying a word, just the occasional squeeze and the look of love that followed.

By now they were a few miles out and the city looked even prettier, if that was possible, with the majestic beauty of Mt. Rainier off to the south. It was said *that the mountain never looked the same twice; it sure couldn't look better to them than at this moment. After crossing Elliott Bay, the ferry began to wind its way through the straights to reach Bremerton. The shore and hillsides were dotted with homes, all uniquely designed with one more beautiful than the other. He broke the silence first.*

*"I doubt if anyone in all those homes could be as happy as I am now."*

*"Me too, Burgie, I hope you won't be disappointed in our home, it's not very big. You will probably have to sleep on the couch in the front room. My sister is three years younger than I am, but quite immature and my older brother Rick is extremely protective –"*

*Interrupting her, he says "Will you stop? I feel nervous enough meeting them for the first time, at Christmas, no less."*

*"I told them how wonderful you are, I know they will just love you."*

"Now I really am nervous. You do have a way of exaggerating my few good qualities."

"Don't be foolish. You are great. Did I tell you my father is a little suspicious of my boyfriends - but he warms up after an hour or so."

"Great, a protective older brother, a suspicious father and an immature younger sister! What did I get myself into?"

"Mom makes up for all our faults. She will make you feel at home right off the bat. The true test is if she baked is homemade bread. And you know you are really in if she baked apple strudel, that's the final seal of approval."

"It will sure be a lot worse on my parents, this is my first Christmas away, and being an only child. They thought it was great with me home for Thanksgiving but the last day or two it sure got sad. I guess I did the right thing switching with Phil so he and Jan could take their new baby home for its first Christmas. He didn't even say thank you, but Jan was so appreciative she almost cried. Well, they are home now and I am lucky enough to be sharing the holiday with your family. Mom told me to call collect on Christmas so she could thank your folks. It made it a lot easier on her knowing I was going to be with someone Christmas Day."

"I hope you are not disappointed, Burgie."

"There is no way I could be disappointed. Your family is so thoughtful to have me over. I hope I don't disappoint them."

"I love you, Burgie."

"I love you, too, dear."

Just as they kissed, the speaker announced that the boat would be docking in 15 minutes and the drivers should return to their cars. They retraced their path, down the steps in the narrow passageway to the lower deck. They found the car and slid in next to each other on the front seat. They reviewed the map and had at least a few minutes before they docked. They held each other closely, kissing and snuggling in the warmth of the car after the cool wind on the upper deck.

"**THUD!**" An older deckhand knocked on the hood and in a laughing voice said, "Hey! We want you to pay attention driving off the ramp to the pier. Keep your mind on the road. Don't want to have to fish you out of the bay," adding cheerfully, "And by the way, Merry Christmas."

Easily embarrassed, Margo responded, with a blushed face, "Merry Christmas to you, sir."

As they left the ferry, they smiled and waved to the deckhand. Going through the small city of Bremerton, he saw the first road sign:

"Well, there's Route 3, we have to follow it to Route 108, and then pick up Route 12 to Aberdeen and points west," he added, "I really enjoyed the ferry ride, especially the part just before we drove out."

"Burgie, you are something. I am so glad we met at the Spanish Castle. You have made this a special Christmas."

He jokingly suggested, "You better watch the maps, or we won't make it by Christmas."

The city of Bremerton quickly gave way to the forest. In places, the trees were so thick the sun could not penetrate the foliage left on the evergreens and pines. In some stretches the trees actually touched over the road, forming a tunnel.

He is jolted back to reality by the announcement over the ships PA:

"We will be docking in 15 minutes. Drivers please return to your cars."

## **SHEPHERD FIELD ON THE PACIFIC COAST**

Bill is on the phone with the OMNI office: "We're real close. Rick has set us up with a chopper to Pacific Shores, but Jack still has a head start." --- "What? This connection isn't that good. Did you say Carpenter told you about someone who lives in Pacific Shores that may help us and you are trying to contact them to see if they will intercept Jack?" The voice on the other ends confirms the comment. Bill replies, "Terrific, God I hope so, keep us updated."

Rick calls back from the cockpit: "We are less than fifteen minutes from Shepherd Field. Tom and I are going to be busy up here; would you make sure everything is secured in the galley? I mean real secure. This runway is barely three-hundred-and-fifty feet longer than our minimum, we will be stopping in an extremely short distance. Swivel your chairs so you are facing the back of the plane to help absorb the stop."

Bill tells the office, "I better get off the line. We're going to land soon."

Doc calls to Rick, "How is this going to compare to the take off?"

Rick calls back, "It will be tricky. They just informed me that the runway is not completely dry yet, so the brakes may not hold in places. We have reverse thrusters on the engines, but I also need the brakes."

Doc is just getting seated when he adds, "Just like the carriers you used to land on."

Rick replies, "Believe me, and wish I had that cable today. I better cut the chatter and pay attention to business up here. We are going to make a low pass over the field to check for obstructions so I can get as low, and slow, as possible on the final approach. Hang on."

After making a very low initial pass over the runway, Rick flies in a long oval and starts on his final approach to the small runway. He takes the Grumman just over the tree tops at the end of the runway, touching down within a few feet from the beginning to maximize the distance left to stop. The reverse thrusters kick in and the brakes are applied at the same time. Bill and Doc are pressed deeply into the backs of the swivel chairs as the crew tries desperately to stop the craft.

Occasionally, the wet pavement causes one of the wheels to slip, losing breaking power on that side causing the plane to occasionally lurch and veer off the center of the runway. Even with the galley secured, the dishes and silverware can be heard shifting around in the drawers and cabinets. Finally, they come to a halt. In the hands of a lesser pilot, the plane would never have stopped in time.

Rick from the cockpit, "Hey, you guys. Is everyone all right back there?"

Bill jokingly replies, "We're fine. Glad you caught the last wire in time."

"I'll taxi over close to the chopper, so you can get on your way to Pacific Shores. Keep us informed as you go."

Rick lets Tom taxi to the waiting chopper, so he can come back before the plane is completely stopped. As soon as the plane comes to a halt Rick starts to let the stairs down, so they can get off in a hurry. As the door opens, Doc and Bill can hear the chopper blades.

Rick tells them, "This is as far as we go. Good luck. Hope you get to Jack in time."

# BURTON'S DRIVE FROM BREMERTON TO THE COAST

The ferry PA announces again that the drivers should return to their cars. Jack retraces his path down to the lower deck of the ferry and finds the car. The deckhands direct the cars off the ferry into the fog shrouded city. Barely a building is visible, even though the street goes through the middle of Bremerton. He finds the road through town that intercepts the main highway to Aberdeen.

The fog begins to break about half-an-hour out of town. The sky is not visible yet, but it is becoming increasingly bright, the first signs that the fog is lifting. He drives for an hour or so and decides to pull off at a road side tourist area with vending machines, tables and a water fountain.

The simple act of getting out of the car clearly defines each sore muscle. He takes his bag from the back seat and walks over to a picnic table. Going through the contents and removes some pain pills. Pouring out two pills he walks over to the water fountain. He thinks to himself, *Taking pain pills now is like a kamikaze pilot worrying about the paint job on his plane.*

He walks back over to the table and removes Margo's picture from his bag. He stands there staring at every detail. It was taken on a clear day, in contrast to the fog he is driving in now. The true beauty of the Point Defiance Park in Tacoma and the Puget Sound in the backdrop only further punctuated her beauty.

Glancing around to first confirm his privacy, he then removes several folded hand towels from the travel bag. Each is unfolded and laid side by side on the table, revealing the six major component pieces of a Glock pistol. It's the one Bill noted as missing from his weapon display in the condo earlier today. It had been disassembled and checked as regular luggage to escape possible detection in the boarding area. Once reassembled, he slides a clip of ammunition into the handle and wraps the weapon in a single towel. Then places it in the bottom of the bag, covering it with the other towels then places Margo's picture on top and closes the bag.

With that task accomplished, he spends a few minutes walking around the rest area to try to loosen up his muscles. The relief of moving around, combined with the initial effects of the pills, should make the last half of his trip more comfortable. There's a large Washington State map under glass for tourist information. He finds his current position on the map and determines it's about forty-five minutes to the ocean, then north along the coast to Pacific Shores.

He spends a few more minutes walking around the rest area to get all the exercise he can before climbing back into the car to continue his journey.

## **DOC AND BILL LEAVE SHEPHERD FIELD FOR PACIFIC SHORES**

Doc and Bill scurry down the stairs of the Grumman to the waiting Medivac. Earlier, when Rick set up the flight, he briefed the pilot that Doc and Bill were headed for Pacific Shores. The pilot reassured Rick that he was familiar with that location and other small towns along the coast.

The pilot introduces himself to Doc and Bill while they are buckling up. Adding, "Mr. Lee has already told me you are headed for Pacific Shores, and in a hurry, is that correct?"

Bill replies "That is correct".

The small helicopter lifts off the grass, rotates north, and immediately heads directly for the ocean coastline. Once over the water, the pilot drops to 100 feet and hugs the shoreline heading northward towards Pacific Shores. The fog has moved inland just enough to make the small towns along the shoreline visible.

After two-and-a-half hours of opulence and comfort aboard the Grumman, Doc and Bill have a hard time getting oriented to the small, noisy craft.

Once they have started down the coast, Bill asks the pilot, "How long will it take us to get to Pacific Shores?"

"Should be just under an hour."

Doc inquires, "Do these small towns have heliports?"

"Not really, I'll put you down on the beach, less than three-hundred feet from town."

## **BURTON ARRIVES AT PACIFIC SHORES**

It has been a long drive from the rest stop, but he is starting to feel better. It must be the combined effect of the bright clearing sky and the medication. The sun highlights his view of Mt. Olympus, ahead and off to the north.

Arriving at the Pacific Ocean, he turns north on Route 109, which runs parallel to the ocean. Trees line both sides of the highway; occasionally, through a clearing, he catches a glimpse of the shoreline off to his left.

There are several small towns and an RV park along his 40 mile route to Pacific Shores. Some home-sites are announced only by a mail box along the road with a gravel path that winds back through the woods. The small towns are usually preceded by an occasional home here and there. Then they become closer together and you come upon two or three businesses followed again by a few scattered homes on the other side that quickly disappear in the rear view mirror, surrendering again to the woods.

The only constant is the line of utility poles, about 300 feet apart, running along the right side of the highway, delivering electricity and telephone service.

After almost an hour, he finally comes to the sign he has been looking for, "Welcome to Pacific Shores." He hasn't been back since that Christmas many years ago. Like the others, the town is built on both sides of the highway. Surprisingly, it has not changed that much, he can still recognize most of the structures. After passing a few businesses, the road makes a sharp right turn at the bakery. Within 200 feet, a sharp left brings him back parallel to the ocean. The cemetery is on his left, between the ocean and the road. He pulls over, hesitates for a minute, then retraces his path to the bakery. Turning off the highway, he drives past the bakery continuing on the road towards the ocean, less than 600 feet straight ahead. The road has been paved all the way to the end since his last visit.

The road ends in a "T", less than 150 feet from the beach. He turns right and drives along behind the homes between the street and the ocean. Most have been built since his last visit. Some are full time dwellings while others are seasonal beach houses. He continues to the beach house at the end of the road, the one he and Margo visited so many years ago, it has weathered well.

Parking in the turn-around, he walks up the small dune that the house is on and then around to the front. The view is spectacular; the ocean is less than 100 yards away, punctuated by the occasional clump of dune grass. Looking back toward the city, he can barely make out the house he visited that holiday. By some standards it would be considered small, but the warmth and genuine friendship that the family shared with him that Christmas went far beyond any physical limitation. He starts to recall that day.

*Margo had joined him for the ride from Tacoma to Pacific Shores on Christmas Eve. They barely got out of the car when Margo's family came out to greet them. The rest of the evening was spent eating an early dinner and sitting around the table discussing each other's backgrounds and their plans for the New Year.*

*He felt at home from the first moment the family had greeted them. Burgie and Margo were tired from the drive and the evening had passed quickly. Bed time came early that Christmas Eve. There were not enough beds, so he slept on the couch in the living room.*

*Margo started to apologize for the sleeping arrangements while she was getting the bedding and making up the couch.*

*Burgie interrupted her, "Your family has made me feel at home. I am sure my folks couldn't have wished for me to have a better Christmas. This is one Christmas I shall never forget."*

*By this time the family had retired to their bedrooms and they were alone in the living room. They indulged in a warm embrace and a long kiss.*

*Burgie suggested with a smile, "Perhaps you would care to join me?*

*Margo responded with a devilish smile, "Are you scared of the night?"*

*"I need someone nearby,"*

*"Someday I'll remind you of this moment."*

*Despite Mom giving everyone strict orders to let Burgie sleep in Christmas morning, Mary, Margo's little sister, woke him early, reminding him that he played several games of chess with Rick last night and had promised to play a game or two with her today. Hearing her from the kitchen, Margo quickly came to his aid.*

*"Mary, Mom said that she wanted Burgie to sleep in this morning.*

*Burgie laughingly commented, "I did promise her I would play today, guess I forgot to say what time. Mary, you find the chess board while I freshen up, and we'll play a few games."*

"Sorry, Burgie, she can be a brat sometimes; what a way to start the day."

"Did you forget, I am an only child and welcome the opportunity to be with your entire family, and that certainly includes Mary."

Margo gave him a big hug, "Speaking of the day – Merry Christmas, Burgie."

"Now, that's the way to start the day. Merry Christmas to you, also."

"You are so nice. In fact, Mom and I were in the kitchen this morning discussing what a great guy you are. She and dad are impressed; even Rick thinks you are a good guy!"

"Now I know why you let me sleep in, so you guys could compare notes."

"Better get freshened up; I put clean towels and a washcloth in the upstairs bathroom. Rick brought your suitcase up to my room last night. It's across the hall from the bathroom."

"So, my suitcase got to stay in your room last night."

"Yes, and it was a perfect companion. Now, you better freshened up. Mary will be down with the chess set any minute."

They had a light breakfast, just enough to hold them until the early Christmas dinner. The table conversation was more relaxed. Yesterday was mostly bringing each other up to date on their background; today was more about current events and personal activities. And, of course, in good humor, several comments from family members reminding Margo of some embarrassing experiences during her childhood.

She bantered back in good humor, reminding them of some of their embarrassing moments. There was a sense of love and respect between the family members.

The rest of the morning and early afternoon was spent watching TV, *punctuated by the occasional board game or two. In fact, Rick, Margo's protective older brother, had taken a liking to him and her little sister Mary really wasn't a brat after all. Her mom and dad had determined, although not openly at first, that he was the first young man that they fully approved of. All in all, he had made a hit with the entire family.*

*The day passed quickly. Before they realized it, Mom was calling everyone to the dinner table.*

*She and Margo had prepared every dish you could associate with the perfect Christmas dinner. The food was delicious, the table chatter was mostly complimenting the ladies on their culinary ability. Everyone was stuffed after sampling every dish several times. Dinner and dessert finally ended and the dishes were being cleared when Rick jokingly commented.*

"Well, Burgie, how did you like the couch?"

"It was great; you should see what I sleep on every night at the barracks."

Margo asked Rick, "Do you really have to go to the radio station today, on Christmas?"

"Yeah, I don't have enough seniority to get the day off, maybe next year." After a moment he continued, "Why don't you and Burgie go down to the beach and check out the summer house. I haven't been out there in a few weeks and we like to keep an eye on it since it is shut down for the winter."

"Would you like to do that later, Burgie?"

"Sure, where is it?"

"Margo will show you how to get there. We left the power on, but the thermometer is set low, you better start a fire to take the chill off. Tune me in and I will play some songs just for the two of you."

"Thanks, we'll be listening."

Burgie exclaimed, "Man, our own private disc jockey!"

"Well, I better take off for the station. See you later. Don't forget to tune me in, Margo."

"You can count on it".

Knowing that Margo would say no, Mary asked Burgie, "Can I go, I won't get in the way. Please, Burgie?"

Burgie hesitates. "Welllllll..."

Margo answered for him, "No way! You have been pestering him all day."

Mom, "Mary you help with the dishes. Let Margo and Burgie have some time to themselves."

"Thanks, Mom."

Looking out the window, Dad commented, "You two better get going. The weather is starting to change and you don't want to get stuck on the beach road if it rains."

"How about it, Burgie, are you ready?"

"I'm ready, and a walk along the beach would be great after this fantastic dinner." Turning to Mom he asked, "Are you sure there isn't anything we can do around here?"

Dad reassured them. "No, you get going. We can take care of everything. Dessert seconds will be ready by the time you get back."

Mom added, "Take care now."

Margo replied, "See you later. Come on Burgie, and don't forget your coat."

They drove through town and turned at the bakery, just like he did today, continuing to the beach road that starts at the end of the bakery parking area. In appearance, it was, at best, a questionable surface. Actually, it was a stable rock road, but a light layer of sand had blown over most of the surface, leaving only a few rocks exposed. For the first-time driver, it was a bit unnerving to venture out on a surface that seemed to be waiting for a victim. Burgie was concerned they would get stuck.

Burgie, with trepidation in his voice, "Are you sure this is a road?"

Margo reassured him. "There is a lot of gravel underneath. The sand is only on the surface. We shouldn't get stuck."

His reluctance was quickly overcome when he drove off the asphalt parking lot and realized the car was not sinking.

Coming to the area where he had to turn he asked, "There are several beach homes; which one is yours?"

"Just a short drive, ours is the farthest one, at the end of the road on the bluff."

"These are really nice places, and right along the beach."

"Ours is certainly not the biggest, hope you like it."

"Is that it up there?" He asked, pointing to the structure at the end of the road.

"That's it; we built it before the road was stabilized. Rick's pickup kept getting stuck so we had to haul all the material up the bluff."

"You hauled it up?"

Margo answered with pride in her voice, "We sure did, this was a family project."

He stopped the car in a small turnaround behind the house. They got out and she continued as they walked up the small hill to the back of the beach house. "Rick and Dad worked construction before Dad was hurt three years ago."

Burgie had never seen anything like it. The single-storey beach house *was built right on the sand, less than one hundred yards from the ocean.*

*"This place is beautiful. Your family really built it?"*

*"Wait until you see it from the inside."*

*She opened the back door, and they walked in. The front wall gave a commanding view of the ocean through ten-foot-high windows, running twenty feet each way from a centered fireplace, made from large river rock. The room was dominated by a massive conversation pit that semi-circled the fireplace, facing the ocean. The kitchen was along the far wall, with three bedrooms and two baths along the back. He was literally speechless. After taking in the ocean view and the interior his first comment was, "This is absolutely beautiful. The front wall is all windows."*

*"Dad and Rick got the windows from a store that was being torn down in Hoquiam. Then we planned the house*

around the windows and fireplace. Everyone worked together. We started in the spring and finished just before Thanksgiving of my freshman year in high school."

"I can't believe you did such a beautiful job. This looks like a travel poster for beach-front property. I mean, this is great!"

"Help me get some wood from the outside rack, and we'll start a fire."

"I'll get the wood, you better build the fire; I never started one in a fireplace."

"You really are from the city. Everyone around here has a fire going to take off the chill."

He went outside and gathered firewood from the storage rack. Coming back in, he walked over to the large windows where she was standing next to the fireplace, looking at the ocean. Placing the wood next to the fireplace, he walked up behind her. Circling his *arms around her slender waist, he gently squeezed her to him while kissing the back of her neck. She turned and put her arms around him. They spent several moments in a deep, sensual kiss with their bodies pressed tightly against each other.*

*He made the first comment, "I brought in the wood, fire-maker. You just got me warmed up; now let's see you get the house warm. I have some other ideas on getting warm."*

*Margo responded with a smile, "Like on the ferry?"*

*"Well, yeah, something like that."*

*"First, let me get the fire going. Would you get Rick on the radio? I think he's on 100.7 FM."*

*She started building the fire while it took him a few minutes to find Rick's radio station.*

*"Here he is. This is something! Having dinner with a disc jockey and*

then listening to him later. Hey, Rick is talking about us."

"The next songs are for two special people; Burgie and Margo. Hope they like these selections,"

The first song started, "Our Winter Love". Placing the extra logs on the rack he walked over to the fireplace. They stood, hand–in–hand, watching the fire start to crackle and adding warmth to the already romantic mood. Embracing, they squeezed each other closer while indulging in a long kiss.

After a few minutes, without a word, they slowly walked over to the soft cushioned conversation-pit couch. Their hands discovered every feature of their partner's body. The mood quickly became sensual; she offered no resistance as he slid her ski sweater over her head. Her eyes conveyed the look of a willing, if not anxious, participant welcoming his advances. Every action and emotion took them to a new sexual threshold.

*What started a few minutes ago as an awkward exploratory encounter had quickly taken a life of its own. Before long their entangled, partially clothed bodies looked for a more comfortable position to continue toward the task at hand. He started to slide off her jeans when she whispered, in a tone so low it was almost like she didn't want him to hear, or stop.*

*"Burgie, we said we would wait."*

*He hesitated for a moment, despite every fiber in his being demanding he continue, at least until she offered some physical resistance. Her eyes conveyed an unspoken message of trust, and he did not violate that confidence.*

*After a moment, he slid off the couch. Sitting on the floor next to her; he held her hand and with resignation in his voice softly acknowledged her comment.*

"You're right, I am sorry, it never should have gone this far."

"It's as much, if not more, my fault; I almost encouraged you by not resisting early on."

"This is really crazy; I didn't want this to happen. I mean, I do want this to continue, but I really do love you."

"Thank you, I almost gave in."

With a hint of laughter in his voice, "Great, now you tell me, I wanted this moment from the first time we went out. No, actually, from the first time I saw you at the Spanish Castle."

"We will watch out for each other from now on,"

"There's something I want to tell you. I spent a lot of time during my leave thinking about you, or, should I say, us. I'm getting out of the Army in February and have to go back to Chicago. While on leave, I contacted Mr. Stein, the registrar at Illinois Institute of

*Technology. It took some convincing, considering my pathetic first two years, but, he finally agreed to see me. We discussed the positive effect the Army has had and my new-found commitment to achieving a degree. I must have been convincing, because he decided to allow me to return this fall."*

*"That's great."*

*"However, it comes with a catch; I must follow a very demanding class schedule that puts me on a track to get my degree in two years."*

*"I am sure you will succeed."*

*"You have eighteen months left to finish nursing school. I know this sounds crazy, but would you consider marrying me after we get out of school?"*

*"Oh, yes, Burgie! I will, I will."*

*"I don't have an engagement ring. I really didn't know until a minute ago that I was going to suggest this today."*

"I don't need a ring. All I want is you."

"Are you sure? I really don't have much to offer, at least not now. After I finish school and get a good job, we can get married."

"I don't need material things, we have each other and that's more than enough for me."

"I've never felt this happy before. All the guys think this is going to be a sad moment; you know giving up running around and all. The truth is, when you find the right person, it's like gaining a new life, not giving one up.

Margo stated, with enthusiasm, "School will be a lot easier with a goal at graduation."

"I told my folks about you and how our relationship inspired me to go back to college. They really want to meet you. Hey, let's plan on you coming to Chicago next Christmas."

"That would be wonderful; I'd love to meet them."

They snuggled into each other's arms in front of the fireplace as Rick's selection of romantic ballads continued with "Chances Are", "The Twelfth of Never", and "Wonderful, Wonderful", all by Johnny Mathis.

Later, as the songs ended and the logs turned to glowing embers, they went for a walk along the beach. The sea started to pick up and she suggested they close up the house and head back before the rain closed the beach road. In the car going back, she sat close alongside him with her arm over his shoulder.

"Burgie, you have made me the happiest person in the world."

"We have a long road ahead, but I know we will travel it together."

"The enjoyment is as much in the journey as the destination."

"I knew you were the smart one."

"Let's come back here to the summer house and make mad passionate love on our tenth wedding anniversary to celebrate this day."

"Why wait ten years? We can go back and celebrate now."

"Burgie, we made a promise."

"Yeah, but I thought it would be worth a try."

She squeezed his shoulders and gave him a big kiss on the cheek.

"Hey, if you do that once more I'll turn around."

"I better not tempt fate. Have you ever driven on the ocean beach?"

"Are you crazy? We'll get stuck!"

"Sacredly cat. We didn't get stuck coming here did we?"

"Well, you are right about that; but we drove on sand over a road, not the beach."

Urging him on, "Instead of turning toward the bakery, just turn the other way, straight toward the ocean. The *gravel should still be under the sand all the way to where the surf has the beach wet. It's that dark gray section about thirty feet wide, where the surf comes up. The wet sand will support the car."*

*"Are you sure? I really don't want to get stuck."*

*"I don't want to walk back, either. It will work, but you have to keep moving until we get to the wet beach area."*

*As they approached the gravel road, Margo prodded him on, "Here's the turn, go toward the beach."*

*"Well, if you are sure, let's go for it."*

*He turned toward the beach and was surprised when the sandy gravel road stayed firm all the way to the wet beach surface.*

*"Hey this is neat, I can I drive along this area just behind the surf?"*

*"See, I told you so."*

*"Man, I never felt anything like this. The sand is really firm where it's wet."*

*With newfound confidence, he continued for at least a mile before finding enough wet sand to turn around. Getting braver on the way back, he cut into the edge of the surf, causing a large spray to come up and curl over the car. Their beach drive was ended when a soft rain started and they retreated to the sand-and-gravel road.*

He is brought back to reality by the sound of children laughing as they run along the beach. He watches for a few minutes as their father runs along with them, helping them get their kite airborne.

He wonders, 'Why the hell didn't we stay married, we could have had children.' It is too late now to consider such pleasures. Returning to the car he retraces the road back past the bakery. This time he drives through the parking lot to the road continuing around the corner to the cemetery.

## **DOC AND BILL ON BOARD THE MEDIVAC**

It's been over half an hour since they left Sheppard Field. An eerie silence has taken command of the cabin. The only sound is the engine and helicopter blades. Doc and Bill are lost in their thoughts while looking out the windows at the beautiful coast line as they fly low over the water.

Doc breaks the silence, "It would be a shame to come this far and not be able to help Jack."

"I sure hope whoever they contacted can reach him in time."

Doc calls forward to the pilot, "How much farther to Pacific Shores?"

"About thirty minutes at most."

"Thanks, is the weather clear ahead?"

"The latest weather advisory said clear along the coast, all the way to Canada."

After a moment, silence returns. The only movement occurs when Doc or Bill check their watches to calculate how much time is left before they arrive at Pacific Shores.

## **PACIFIC SHORES CEMETERY**

The cemetery is beautifully maintained, as only happens in a small town where everyone cares. On an average day it is occupied by five, or at the most, ten people, usually local residents, visiting the grave sites. However, today it is crowded; it is a tradition in small towns that Memorial Day is a special time when past generations of families and long forgotten friends have all come together to visit grave sites. They plant flowers and renew old friendships while catching up on what happened since their last visit.

This Memorial Day is no exception, with at least sixty people representing all age groups from newborn through great grandparents.

A wheelchair is being pushed by a woman in her late 20's with a small child alongside. They occasionally pause and exchange greetings as they move through the people. They stop, and the younger woman goes back to a van to get some flowers. There is nothing familiar or unusual about anyone in particular that catches his attention. No one stands out; in fact, they blend into a moving profusion of colors, shapes, sizes and ages.

He sits in the car for a few minutes, just taking in the view of the small cemetery with the ocean as a backdrop, enjoying the muffled sound of the surf. Reaching down on the floor behind the front seat he grasps the leather travel bag and pulls it over the seat, placing it next to him. He looks around; making sure no one is nearby. Only then does he open the bag. He takes Margo's picture out of the flight bag and spends a few moments examining every detail of the beautiful young woman standing on the tree stump. Then, almost with reverence, he slides it into one of the large pockets of his bush jacket. He lifts out the loose towels used to disguise the additional contents. He takes one more look around, then lifts out the Glock pistol he assembled at the rest area. Holding it low, so no one will see, he slides the barrel back and forth advancing a bullet from the clip into the chamber. The weapon is now ready to fire. He slips it into the other large lower front pocket of his bush jacket.

He exits the car and walks over to the grave site directory. He runs his finger down the alphabetical list, stopping at a particular name and the corresponding grave site location.

Checking the cemetery layout map he finds the aisle and site. As he walks toward the aisle, he is greeted with a cordial "hello" or "good afternoon" by almost everyone he passes. Usually the residents would recognize everyone in the cemetery, but this is Memorial Day weekend and they assume he is a former resident coming back to visit a grave site, so he passes among them without concern. It would certainly be cause for alarm if they had any idea of the reason for his visit.

Approaching the aisle he hears a strained, and yet vaguely familiar voice, somehow singled out from all the background chatter. She calls faintly. "Hello, Burgie."

He is caught off guard. Instinctively he turns toward the voice and, without realizing, impulsively reaches in his pocket for the gun. Who could possibly recognize him from his single visit so long ago?

She calls again, this time stronger, "Burgie."

He scans in the general direction of the call; it's difficult to identify her location with all the background noise.

At that moment she calls again, "Over here, Burgie."

This time he hones in on the source and realizes it is coming from an older woman in a wheel chair next to a bench at the end of the aisle he selected.

It takes a second or two to register. Then he realizes the last time he saw her she was much younger and full of life that Christmas weekend, its Margo's mother.

He was so single-minded in his mission that he never thought of encountering someone who might recognize him. He relaxes his grip on the gun and removes his hand from his pocket. He just stands there, not knowing what to say. His expression changes from surprise at seeing an old friend to one of anxiety and frustration. He recalls their last emotional conversations when he was trying to locate Margo. That was several months after Margo returned home from her Christmas visit to Chicago to meet his parents.

Her opening comments described clearly that the meeting was not by chance. In an older but firm voice she says, "I know you probably don't want to talk, but some people from your company called and asked me to try to reason with you. They have no idea, nor do you, what really happened over thirty years ago." She looks at him with kind, familiar eyes. "Please, sit down on the bench and give me a chance to explain."

This is a family that brought him so much happiness and then crushed his world. The last thing he needs is for her to drag up the past, but for some unknown reason, maybe it's the look of remorse on her face, he reluctantly sits down. He cannot conceal his feelings. His face still betrays his anxiety; his voice openly conveys his hostility.

"What the hell was the masquerade for? I didn't know until a few days ago what really happened. The last tape she sent was within a few months after her visit to meet my parents, she made it quite clear that she had been married and left the state."

Without realizing, his voice is becoming louder, to the extent that several people have taken notice and are becoming concerned over this strangers conduct. Concerned for her safety, one of the neighbor men has begun to walk toward them. She motions that everything is OK. The neighbor returns to his family; but keeps an eye on the situation.

Burgie continues, with disgust in his voice, "I called repeatedly and you told me she did not want me to know where she was living. I must have called you at least a dozen times before I finally accepted the idea that she did not want to have anything to do with me. She said on the tape she could not wait until I finished college and she wanted to start her life now."

He continues, more enraged, "Did she tell you we planned to get married after we finished school? We made that vow at your summer place, right over there." He points to the beach house. "We repeated it the following Christmas when Margo came to Chicago to meet my parents. She said she would wait! I spent my whole life loving and hating her at the same time. I drove my way to the top at OMNI to prove I was worth waiting for. I even hoped she would see my pictures on magazines and read the stories of my success over the years and regret what she did!"

He pauses for a moment, and then continues. "I was married, to probably the most understanding woman in the world, and it didn't last two years because I was consumed with my quest for achievement. I lost a lifetime trying to prove that Margo would regret not waiting. All that time, she never called or wrote, so last month I hired a private investigator to locate her, only to find out she was never married. What the hell really happened?"

His voice has again become loud, and again the concerned neighbor has to be reassured with a nod from Mom that everything is all right. Mom sits patiently, allowing him to vent his frustration. Now, she carefully removes an old-fashioned Webcor tape recorder from the bag on her lap.

"Do you recognize this, Burgie?"

His answer is swift and reflects his anger. "Sure I do, I worked my butt off as a bartender while going to college to buy one for each of us, so we could tape classes and send tapes back and forth instead of writing. I left mine in a plane at the bottom of Lake Michigan last Friday." Sarcasm now enters his tone. "She also used that to record her final message to me, my 'Dear John'. Did you save it as a reminder of her deceit, or did she want you to give it back to me, just to rub it in? I loved her - for Christ sake, I still do."

"I kept this recorder a secret for all these years. No one knew I had it. The first time I played it was on the way over here. It has a tape that will best explain what really happened. Margo made it for you. It was recorded a few months after she came back from visiting with you and your parents. I made a deal with her to leave you a message to explain what happened in the event something went wrong. She, no we, thought we were doing the right thing at the time. I have wrestled with my conscience for all these years, please forgive us".

"Why the hell should I listen to this tape now, after all these years? It can't possibly explain the deception, or start to resolve the betrayal and hatred I have felt."

He stops, looking away for a moment, thinking to himself, *I can't imagine anything that can make it better now. I never should have stopped to talk with her. A few minutes ago I sat in the car and finally, after all these years, felt some sense of relief and finality to my life. I have only added grief by listening to her.*

Turning back to Mom, he practically screams, "I've had enough, let me get on with my task."

"Please, Burgie! Listen to the tape before you do anything. It can't resolve the past, but it can give you a reason for wanting a future. You'll realize you do have a lot to live for, just listen to her message first, please!"

She pushes the play button as she hands him the tape player. It starts one of their favorite songs, "Where or When" by the Letterman,

For a moment he remembers playing that song and several others on the jukebox in the coffee shop at Midway Airport the Christmas Margo came to Chicago to meet his parents. He is jolted back to full consciousness when he hears Margo's unmistakable voice once more.

*"Dearest Burgie, Mom made me record this tape as part of our agreement. I really don't know if you will*

*ever hear this message. I don't know what has happened for her to decide to give this to you. I have to trust her judgment. My God, I just realized I don't even know how old you are now.*

*This is terribly confusing for me. I hope you never hear this tape, so you won't hate me for what I have done. Yet, I feel awful not being with you, especially at this moment. I am so sorry; I just didn't want to burden you with this situation. I am so confused, talking to a machine with a message I want so much to tell you in person. I want to go over to the phone and call you, but it wouldn't be fair to you.*

*I planned so many things for us to do, only to find out the best and worst news of my life in less than a week. That was last March, after I came home from visiting your family. It is now Christmas Day and I am at the summer house. My memories are of last Christmas with your family, and the one before that*

> when you came to my house to meet my family. Remember Rick playing 'Our Winter Love' for us? I am sitting on the couch looking at the ocean with a fire to take off the chill. I can still feel the warmth of your arms and will never forget how happy you made me that day, and every day after. I always have, and always will, love you, you must believe that."

Her voice starts to crack; he can tell she is about to cry:

> "The bad news I got last March was that I have cancer. I have been lucky to make it this far, but the cancer is going to win out soon. I feel so lonely without you, but I have chosen this course and do hope that you do not hate me for it."

He pushes the stop button. He's almost in tears, but there is still rage in his tone: "I called so many times! Why didn't you tell me so we could have at least had those last months together? Did she really think so little of me that she didn't want to be a burden? Christ, Mom, I loved her. I still do. Why didn't she let me know?" Mom does not answer. She simply reaches over and pushes the play button again.

> "I am lonely for you, but I am not alone. You see, the good news I got last March was that I was pregnant. Yes, our one indulgence in your basement last Christmas has resulted in the most beautiful little girl right here in my arms. That's right, you are a father. I named her Jackie. She is just two months old and has your electric green eyes. As I look into them now, I can see the mischief just below the surface, just like yours."

He reaches for the stop button on the recorder but Mom takes his hand saying, "Please, let her finish, Burgie. I want her to tell you, before you ask any more questions."

## To Chase a Ghost

Reluctantly he pulls his hand away. Margo continues on the tape.

*"So many things happened at one time. I came home from the Christmas visit, your Mom died in February, and then I got my news in March. I made a decision that seemed so right at the time, but now I am not sure I did the right thing. I decided if I told you I was expecting you would want to raise her after my death. It would be a terrible burden on a young man and his father to raise a newborn, so Mom and I decided not to tell you anything. I am so sorry for deceiving you. I can only imagine the hurt that last tape I sent must have caused. I wish that decision seemed as clear now as it did last March.*

*I question if I made the right choice. Mom and Dad have agreed to raise Jackie, and my sister Mary has been so helpful. I feel so bad for calling her a brat all these years. They have made these last few months bearable. I know this is the right thing to do, yet I wish you could be a part of Jackie's life as much as I wish I could continue. I am punished by the idea that I will look down and see a girl without you as her father, and a wonderful man deprived of having such a beautiful daughter. What seemed right just a few months ago seems impossible to justify now. I have to trust that God will take care of you both. I only hope He can forgive me for what I have done. Wherever we are, Burgie, we will always be together."*

He listens for a second or two to make sure that is the end before stopping the tape. He has tears in his eyes and his first words reflect the confusion on his face. "She never married? I have a daughter?" His expression and voice quickly turn to anger. "Who were you to deny me the opportunity to raise my own daughter? Why didn't you call after Margo died? I never had the opportunity to make that decision. Why didn't you call?"

Mom responds with remorse in her voice. "Burgie, Margo made me promise. Mary was a real help bringing up Jackie. Later on, when you married, we spent months of arguing whether we should let you know. Then, when you divorced so soon, we decided it would be too traumatic for Jackie to be told. She has known only us from birth, and it didn't seem right to put her through the commotion of relocation and adjustment.

"We thought we were doing what was in Jackie's best interest. I made Margo record the tape that Christmas, but I never thought it would turn out this way. Time slipped by and we loved Jackie so much. Before Dad died last year, he made me promise to tell you the truth. I just keep coming up with one reason after another to justify in my own mind not to." She stops for a moment. He can see real regret and pain in her expression. She continues. "It wasn't fair to Jackie or you. I guess I needed her as an emotional tie to Margo."

A young woman has walked up behind him while Mom has been talking. She has been there for several minutes without him noticing her. She has tried to speak a couple times but doesn't know how to start the conversation. Finally her voice from behind him speaks softly, with hesitation and more like an awkward question, "Dad?"

He turns. There is no doubt she is Margo's daughter. If he could find the tree stump at Point Defiance and pose her on it you would swear the photo in his pocket was just taken. Everything about her is Margo, except she has his deep electric green eyes. The last few minutes have boggled his mind and now this discovery, a daughter! All he can say is, "No one has ever called me Dad before."

He starts to get up and she puts her hand on his shoulder as she walks around in front of him saying, "I never called anyone Dad before, either. I'm as surprised as you are. I just heard the tape myself for the first time when we drove over to meet you. Gram and Mary told me you died in the war, so I assumed I didn't have a father."

Burgie, with tears in his eyes, "You look just like your mother. You are beautiful." He looks at Mom. "I'm sorry, I was confused. I just wish I could have been here to raise my little girl."

"Well, Dad – God that sounds strange. I wanted a father so long, and now I finally have one."

"It sounds strange, being called Dad."

Jackie points to a van in the parking lot. "Well, how about father-in-law? My husband Eric is over in that van."

A little girl, cute as a button and at the most four years old, walks up. She instinctively goes over to Jackie. She hugs her mother's leg at the knee, and looks up at him for a moment, then tells her, "I put the flowers on Grandma Margo's grave."

Jackie, looking down at the little girl, "Marguerite, I want you to meet someone, his name is – Burgie."

"Hi, Mr. Burgie", then, with all the innocence of a child she quips, "That's a funny name."

Jackie responds lovingly, "Marguerite, that's not nice. He knew your Grandma Margo."

"I'm sorry, Mr. Burgie. I'm named after Grandma Margo. Will you tell me about her?"

"Please, tell both of us, Dad. Or, should I say, Grandpa?"

Mom suggests, "Why don't you three walk along the beach. You have a lot to catch up on. Eric and I will tell your friends everything is all right. It is all right, isn't it, Burgie?"

Burgie replies without hesitation, "It sure is, Mom; you were right, I now have every reason to live."

He starts to reach in his pocket for the gun then realizes he can't just pull it out to give it to Mom. He stops, then slips off the bush jacket and places it next to Mom on the bench.

"I have something I want you to give to Eric. It's in the jacket pocket. I won't need it, after all."

He lifts Marguerite up in his arms. Jackie puts her arm around his waist and they start down the path to the beach. "Let me tell you about your grandma Marguerite. Where should I start? I remember, it was at the Spanish Castle when I was in the Army a long time ago. I went with some friends, and halfway through the evening I met your grandmother Marguerite. She was the most beautiful girl in the room. We danced every dance the rest of the evening. I knew immediately I was in love."

His words fade quickly against the sound of the surf as they walk toward the ocean.

## THE MEDIVAC WITH DOC AND BILL FLIES OVERHEAD

From down the beach the helicopter carrying Doc and Bill passes low overhead. They recognize Jack. Doc comments, "Looks like he found a lot more than he was looking for."

"Yeah, I'd say the Iceman has melted after all."

## BACK ON THE BEACH

Burgie continues as they approach the beach, "Then I came to your Grandmother Margo's house for Christmas Dinner a long time ago. We visited your beach house just over there and walked along this very beach."

Marguerite notices one kite that stands out from all the rest. "Look, Mr. Burgie, isn't that the most beautiful kite you have ever seen?"

He recognizes the kite immediately; it's just like the one he watched off his balcony a few short days ago. "You're right, it is beautiful." He pauses for a moment, then asks. "Do you know how to fly a kite?"

She looks surprised by the question, "Of course I do, silly."

"If I buy one just like that will you teach me how to fly it?"

## The End

Made in the USA
Charleston, SC
17 February 2017